BOOKS PUBLISH

Black Canvas: A Campus Haunting
Matt Richardson

Sugar: A Memoir of Craving
Samuel Peterson

Breakfast with Unicorns: Poems
Hunter Boone

Trans Imaginations
C. M. Jacqline

Vicissitudes: Love Transforms
Kim Green

American Fascism: How the GOP Is Subverting Democracy
Brynn Tannehill

Tomorrow, or Forever, and Other Stories
Jack Kaulfus

Swimming Upstream: A Novel
Jacob Anderson-Minshall Lou Sullivan

Daring To Be A Man Among Men
Brice D. Smith

Giving It Raw: Nearly 30 Years with AIDS
Francisco Iba ez-Carrasco

Life Beyond My Body: Transgender Journey to Manhood in China
Lei Ming

Below the Belt: Genital Talk by Men of Trans Experience
Edited by Trystan T. Cotten

DEDICATION

For all the Black queer and trans people
making the best of difficult times.

ANGELS

OF

MERCY, LIGHT

AND

FOG

Matt Richardson

Transgress
Press

ANGEL

OF

FOG

2015

Raheed James looked nervously around the room. Every surface of the directors' office was covered with paperwork and files. He noticed that the computer was several years old and the telephone looked like it was from the 1990's with buttons that lit up at the bottom to indicate different lines. There were inspirational posters on the wall. Each one had a slogan and a picture of a landscape or an ocean sunset. His least favorite said, "The Only Guarantee of Failure is to Never Try." He had seen plenty of people work hard all their lives, trying until their bodies gave out and not get very far. Like his aunt.

"You know, Raheed, you just turned 18 last month and thank goodness that we could offer you an extension on your stay here as long as you were in college, but even that is going to expire soon. The state just doesn't have the funds to support people in your situation." The director was an old white guy. Raheed guessed that he was probably crazy old, like 50, but he seemed OK. Like he gave a shit.

"Yeah. I don't know what to do about it." Raheed felt his heart beating at the thought of leaving YouthRight. He had been there for about a year—since he dropped out of high school and got his GED. As far as places for warehousing kids go, it wasn't bad. He had seen some awful foster homes, and this place was clean, they made sure he ate, they supplied him with a bus pass to get to school and work and it was rent-free. But it was all going away because he turned 18. The magic number. He spent all his childhood waiting to be 18 and be all grown up, but he didn't feel grown up, he just felt scared.

"Look. You have a good start. You have a job, you are in community college. You'll be fine."

"Fine? I can barely make it now and I'm not paying rent. I can't take any more hours at the Jack in the Box or I'm going to flunk out of school."

"What about family? Did you patch things up with your aunt?"

Raheed shook his head. His aunt had diabetes and had just spent a few weeks in the hospital with heart issues. She lost a lot of money because she couldn't work during that time and the medical bills were piling up. "They have their own problems, you know. They don't need another mouth to feed. They don't have room anyway."

"Well, we'll find you a halfway house or sober living house you can go to for a while. You need to relax. We'll get this solved."

Raheed wished he was as confident as the director that things were going to work out. "Man, I just need to get some more money. That's what I need."

The director furrowed his eyebrows with concern. "Don't do anything you will regret later." Raheed left without looking back.

Raheed felt his eyes on him. YouthRight always had volunteers from the university that did most of the supervising of the residents on the day-to-day. According to a string of volunteers, the university had a strange requirement that each student do at least 100 hours of community service before they graduate. Something about the founders of the university being missionaries. At first, they all had to go out on missions, but as time had gone on and the university got less Christian, they eventually changed the requirement to be any community service as long as it was a nonprofit. A lot of people apparently still went on missions to the far corners of the world. The people who went to YouthRight were mostly eager young white do-gooders who wanted to fulfill their community service requirement by working with kids. Raheed hated them. They all wanted to be his friend and help him turn him from a life of crime. Some of them wanted to introduce him to Jesus Christ as a personal savior. A few just wanted to hear his terrible story of drugs and abuse. All of them thought that they knew his story before they even met him.

Ben was different. For the most part, he was a typical white frat boy like all the others. He wore expensive, but casual clothes, drove a sports car that most adults couldn't afford after a lifetime of hard work, and walked around like he owned the place. What made him different was that he never said a word to him. He didn't try to beat him in basketball or show that they could be bros by talking about music. Ben stayed mostly with the younger kids and watched Raheed when he thought no one was noticing. He watched Raheed while he was playing ping pong, while he watched TV, when he hung out with the other guys. No matter what Raheed did, he caught Ben looking at him. One time he saw Ben drive up with his girlfriend clutching his arm. He jumped out of his amazing car to drop something off and left the girl in the car. The girlfriend was exactly like Raheed expected, blond, thin, another university student. Ben was what white people call ruggedly handsome. *So why is he sweating me?* Raheed wondered.

One day he decided to find out more about Ben. He was at a table near the basketball court with some other residents and stopped Ben as he walked by, pretending like he didn't care that Raheed was there.

Raheed stopped him. "Hey, you! What's your name? Who's on your shirt?

Ben looked around nervously and walked over to the table. He looked like someone who had been caught shoplifting but was trying to play it off. "Hi, I'm Ben. These are Greek letters. Each one—"

"I know what Greek letters are, Ben, I mean, which ones are they?"

Ben told him his house letters and about how much he loved his house. "We're the best one on campus. What's your name?"

"You got any Black people in your frat?" Another kid yelled out.

"Oh, of course. We have two Black guys, like four Latinos, three Asians. We even have an Arab guy in our house. It's a stereotype that we are all white."

"Wow. A whole 2 Black people!" The other guys at the table laughed. Ben turned red. One of the guys asked, "How white are these Black people? I mean, do you have to pass some sort of white test to get in or what?"

"We are not like those other assholes you've heard about on campus. We respect each other and think that all lives matter."

The group of guys yelled out collectively. "Oh no! He said that shit!" They laughed and waved him away. "All lives! Fuck this white boy."

Ben backed away, afraid that he was going to get jumped. He was also genuinely confused about why the conversation had taken a dive. What? *What did I say?* He thought.

One of the guys walked up to him. "Are you seriously scared right now? Oh man. You're ridiculous. Why would we hurt you? Right here? We would all go to jail, just for being here when it happened."

Ben said nothing and checked for the exits. They all laughed, leaving Ben even more confused.

Raheed stood up and said, "Come on y'all. Let's leave him alone-it's time for group." The young men wandered back inside the building, still laughing. Raheed saw Ben standing alone and still a little scared. He felt sorry for him. "My name is Raheed." He called back to him.

Ben didn't stop shaking until he got back to his room. "I'm so stupid!" He berated himself. Every time he thought about Raheed and the other guys at the youth home making fun of him, he wanted the ground to swallow him up whole. He wanted the first time he talked to Raheed to be different. Ben wanted it to be fun and relaxed, not be a laughingstock. He laid down on his bed and covered his face with his pillow. He hadn't felt this embarrassed since Lindsey Baxter told the whole 6th grade that she didn't want to kiss him because he had lice. Up until that moment, he had had a crush on her and fantasized about her every night before he went to bed. Now it was a Black guy he was supposed to be helping. It started the moment he saw him. Ben signed up to work at YouthRight because several people told him it was easy, and they let you make your own hours. At first, it was fine. He supervised the kids playing kickball and helped serve the lunches. Then he saw Raheed come into the cafeteria. He was tall and brown-skinned, wearing a tank top and it showed his tattoos. He moved with strength and confidence. He sat by himself and pulled out a book. He was studying in the summer! Everybody else was laughing and talking, and Raheed was studying. He asked one of the staff people about him and they told Ben that Raheed was in community college. He left high school, got a GED and immediately started taking classes at the college and working. The staff said he was the model resident and they thought it was too bad he was getting too old to stay.

Ben could not help but think Raheed was beautiful. He could not stop thinking about what he looked like in a tank top. He tried putting him out of his mind and focusing on the kids, but he found himself watching Raheed whenever he was in the same space with him. He would look for him, making excuses to go find pieces of equipment or ask some dumb question he already knew the answer to just to get a glimpse of him. The darkness of his skin and the fullness of his lips made him breathe heavy.

Ben assured himself he wasn't gay. He had a girlfriend, and he never had any problems performing with her. He knew that people sometimes experimented in college. He met his girlfriend his first year and he was faithful to her. It was his sophomore year and he was happy with his life. Except he couldn't stop thinking about Raheed. Back in his room, he took off his jeans and tried to think about his girlfriend, but it was no use. He was thinking of Raheed and his chest. He imagined his tattoos peeking out from underneath his tank top. Those lips. Then a kiss. He slid his hands down his underwear. He could feel Raheed pushing his head down, making his way to his knees, planting small kisses on Raheed's torso on the way down. He unbuckles his pants, kissing the outline of Raheed's hard dick on the fabric of his jeans. He lowers Raheed's pants caressing the inside of his thighs with his tongue until he finds his balls. With one hand, he strokes Raheed's dick while he finds the bottom of his balls with the tip of his tongue. He makes his way to his long, dark shaft, licking it like an ice cream cone until he gets to the tip. In his mind, Raheed tells him to 'say ah' and when he does, pushes his dick forcefully to the back of his throat, filling him up so that he can't breathe. Raheed's hands are on either side of his head as he thrusts himself in Ben's mouth. Ben stays with his mouth wide open, looking up at Raheed until he is forced to pull back in order to breathe. He quickly catches his breath and then takes him in his mouth again, rapidly moving up and down until he hears Raheed let out a loud grunt. He imagines hot cum coating the back of his throat as Raheed stiffens.

Ben came with his own moan, sending cum onto the sheets of his bed. He reached over for some tissues to scoop up the mess and sighed. He was going to have to find a new place to volunteer. He was never going to have Raheed and it was going to drive him crazy to see him all the time. Maybe once he left, this insane obsession would go away, and he would just be happy with his girlfriend. What would his father say? He would call him a faggot, that's what he'd say. His father called all the gay men he knew faggots behind their backs, even his uncle, who was not really a blood relative, but a close friend of his mother's before she died. Ben suspected he called them that to their faces too before he could get sued for it. He closed his eyes and dreamt that Raheed lay at his side.

"How's Auntie?"

Raheed's cousin didn't look up from his phone. "She's good."

"So, when's she coming back?"

"I don't know, man. I think she's doing a double shift at the hospital." His aunt was a patient care tech, which meant that she cleaned up after the nurses and doctors for about $12/hour. If she was pulling a double shift, Raheed knew she must be hard-up for funds. He wondered if he could convince her to let him stay if he gave her his money from Jack in the Box. But if he did that, he would not be able to save for his own room in another apartment. He didn't want to be out on the street. He had seen a lot of kids get stuck there and he wanted to keep going to school.

"OK. Tell your mom I came by."

"For sure, man," his cousin said, still texting. A silver Mercedes turned the corner and parked in front of the house down the street.

"Hey, Cuz, didn't that used to be D'Shawn's old house?"

Finally looking up from his phone, Raheed's cousin said, "Yeah. It still is. I mean, he moved out, but his mama still lives there."

"Then who's car is that?"

"D'Shawn's. He comes by sometimes and gives his moms some money."

"Oh yeah? What's D'Shawn been up to that he's making Benz money?"

"He's been under some white men, that's what."

"He's working for white people? Doin' what?"

"Not what, who. When I say he's under some white men, I mean he's under them. You know," he said sliding one hand flat underneath the other.

"For reals?"

"Remember Fat Dale? But he's always been like that." Raheed remembered. Fat Dale was a guy that owned a corner store a couple of blocks away. Dale had a wife and two grown children who would stop by the store and ask him for money sometimes. All the kids went there to buy candy and sodas. He would get the boys to go into the back with him by promising to give them free stuff. When they got back there, he would give the boys money to rub his hands on their pants. Raheed never went to the back himself, but he heard stories. Dale liked boys from about 12 to 15.

"He used to have that store on Main Street," Raheed said. "I think I looked too old for him to bother me. After you got too old, he didn't mess with you."

"D'Shawn was one of the kids that Fat Dale used to give money to. The other kids did it a few times and stopped. D'Shawn was the only one to keep doing it until Fat Dale told him he didn't want him no more."

Raheed's cousin shook his head at the sad story. Raheed watched D'Shawn walk up to his mother's house with packages. Raheed liked his style. He didn't have on a suit, but his clothes weren't cheap either.

"D'Shawn's up to his old tricks. I heard some white man came to his momma's house looking for him and saying that D'Shawn's his lover. So, I guess he's gay with these old white guys and he gets them to buy him shit. That must pay pretty good. I couldn't do it, though." His cousin said, going back to looking at his phone.

Raheed hung out on the porch for a while even after his cousin went inside. When he saw D'Shawn come out of his mother's house, he flagged him down before he drove off. "Hey! D'Shawn. What's up, man? How are you? Do you remember me? I'm Miss Ella's nephew, Raheed."

"Yeah. The one whose parents died. I remember you. How you been, man?" The two men shook hands.

"Alright. I'm staying at the YouthRight center for a while until I age out."

"Oh yeah. How's your auntie? Is she living up the street?"

"She's doing ok. She's still there. Struggling. How's your mom?"

"Same. She's working hard every day."

"You hungry? You want to catch some lunch? It's not every day I get to see someone from the old neighborhood." At first, Raheed didn't know what he wanted from D'Shawn. He just had a vague idea that he needed money and he didn't want to go to jail and D'Shawn seemed to know how to get money fast without selling drugs. They went to a burger and fish fry place around the corner from D'Shawn's mother's place. The plastic yellow benches and tables and linoleum floors made Raheed remember what it was like when he first came to his aunt's house four years before. D'Shawn was one of the few older guys who took the time to talk with him and make him feel welcome.

"You were always nice to me. I just lost my parents and you were cool. I just wanted to thank you for that." The two sat at one of the three tables in the tiny storefront take-out joint.

"For sure. You liking YouthRight? I hear they're all right over there."

"It's ok, but I to tell you the truth, I got nothing coming out of that place. I'm going to community college right now and I want to go to a four-year university, but I can't afford it. I look at you and your nice car and clothes and I think, how can I save something for school? Or at least not wind up on the streets."

"You want to do what I do?"

"I don't know, man. What do you do? I hear rumors, but I don't put stock into what other people say."

"You know the deal. What's on your mind? You wouldn't be talking to me if you didn't have a plan." Raheed felt D'Shawn sizing him up, seeing if he should trust him.

"There's this guy at the center who is watching me all the time. He's one of the student volunteers and he's loaded, man. I looked him up. His father owns like half the town. I figure I can make some money."

D'Shawn looked at him in the eyes. "Are you ready to fuck this guy? Because robbing him would just land you in prison." He took a long drag of his soda, waiting for Raheed to respond.

Raheed didn't know what to say. "Maybe he can just suck my dick or something. I don't want to touch him."

"There is no such thing as being a little bit pregnant," D'Shawn said, finishing off his sandwich. "You're either hustling or you're not. These men want sex, and they want to pay for it and some of them are downright repulsive, but you've got to think about the payoff."

"So, are you gay now? I mean, I heard you got this guy who you spend time with, but it doesn't sound like you like it. What's up?"

"I used to be much more interested in that question. I don't know if it matters anymore." D'Shawn got up to leave but left Raheed his cell number. "He's young. Sounds like he may be interested in a boyfriend experience. If you want to keep it casual, you approach him with a proposition. Tell him you caught him looking, and if he wants more, he's going to have to pay. Good luck. Tell your aunt I said hi next time you see her. She's been good to my mom."

Raheed watched D'Shawn leave the restaurant. He didn't look like a prostitute. He looked like he was a successful young man. That's what he wanted to look like.

Raheed walked back and forth in the parking lot. "It's ok. It's just for money," he said to himself. "This guy's got a lot of it. OK, OK, I can do this." He stood for a moment to gather his courage. He thought, *I've gotten my dick sucked lots of times, how different can it be?* When he saw Ben get into his car he quickly went over and blocked him from leaving the parking lot. He walked over to the passenger side door.

Ben tried not to stare at Raheed's dick perfectly framed in the car window. "Hey, Raheed, what's up?" he asked trying to be calm, as he rolled down the window, but inside he felt like he was having a small heart attack at the sight of Raheed at his window. Raheed's unexpected presence made Ben shake with fear and desire. He didn't know which one was winning.

Raheed took a deep breath and bent down to look into the window. It was nicer up close. He got in and sat on the soft leather seat before he lost his nerve. "I saw you looking at me," Raheed said with his toughest voice, staring straight ahead.

Ben was shaking outwardly, "I don't know what you're talking about," he said mechanically. "I look at all the residents the same way."

"Aw man, don't give me that shit." Ben's denial made him mad and gave Raheed the push not to be nervous anymore. "Don't lie. I saw you," he said.

16

"It's against the rules…"

"Fuck that. Why don't you own up to the fact that you've been looking at me ever since you got here."

All Ben could manage was to repeat himself. "I don't know what you're talking about. I like all the residents in the program," he said out loud, but he was screaming at himself in his head, trying to come up with something better to say. Ben's hands were on the wheel of the car to keep them from shaking uncontrollably. All he could think was, what if his father found out? Then it occurred to him that Raheed could beat him up. What if his friends were hiding outside the car ready to jump him?

I can't believe this white boy is going to sit here and deny it, Raheed thought. Raheed's anger made him bold. "Do you want to suck my dick?"

"What?" Ben sat mystified. He heard, but he didn't hear. Nothing was making sense.

"You heard me. You can do it for $100."

"You want me to suck your dick?"

"If you will pay," Raheed said looking in Ben's eyes, bolder than ever. What he saw surprised him. *This guy's afraid. He's afraid of doing this*, Raheed thought. Disappointment washed over him. *I did this for nothing. He's probably going to report me.* Raheed realized how close he was to being thrown out of the house. Then where would he go? He started to plan his strategy, *I will lie and say he invited me into my car*, he thought, as he put his hand on the door to go. "Whatever, man," he said to sound tough.

Ben was afraid his chest was going to cave in. Wasn't this what he wanted? All the times he masturbated, he imagined himself swallowing Raheed, making him moan. Even in his fear, he was rising. He saw Raheed grab the handle to the door. His hand seemed to move on its own because the next thing he noticed was that it was on Raheed's shoulder.

"Wait," Ben said. Even though he knew it was his voice, it seemed like someone else was saying it. "Wait," he said again. "I'll do it."

Raheed took his hand away from the door. Everything changed. He no longer had the problem of feeling humiliated that he made the offer. He had a whole new problem. *Now I will have to go through with this*, he thought.

"$100," he repeated like he always got white men to suck his dick for money.

"I have to go to the cash machine," Ben said.

"Let's go."

Ben looked at Raheed and hesitated turning on the car. *I don't have to go through with this*, he thought, but he found himself driving down the familiar streets to his bank. Ben parked and looked at the cash machine and back at Raheed.

Raheed rolled his eyes. "I'm not going to rob you," he said. "Stupid white boy. Why would I rob you? You know where I live. There's a camera right there." He pointed to the bank.

"I'm sorry," Ben said. I've never done this before. Ben got the cash and then got back in the car. "Where do we go?" He asked Raheed.

"I know this spot that's in the cut. Lots of trees and no one is around." Raheed was proud of himself for getting such a good place lined up beforehand.

"You must do this all the time, huh?"

"Just do it and we can end this," Raheed said.

It frightened Ben to find out that he was actually hungry for him. He wanted him so badly that he embarrassed himself by trying to help Raheed pull down his pants. He gave Raheed the money.

I got this, Raheed thought. "Slow down," Raheed said. *Wow,* he thought, *this guy really wants to suck me off.* The thought made him get a semi by the time he had his pants down.

Ben was surprised that Raheed was half-way there when he leaned over and grabbed his dick, and guided it into his mouth. He had tried not to stereotype black men. He knew Raheed wasn't small from the bulge in his pants, but he was big up close. Raheed grew thick and long quickly. He licked the shaft and head, hoping to tease him to full length. Ben was still shaking with fear, but his impatience overtook him and he slipped Raheed's penis into his mouth and down his throat. He surprised himself with how much of Raheed's length he was able to fit into his mouth. Ben closed his eyes and worked up and down the extent of Raheed's broad shaft.

Raheed gasped. He was caught off guard by the warmth and wetness of Ben's mouth. He was rock hard and he resisted moaning with pleasure with every bit of his being. He didn't know where to put his hands. He was used to touching the person who gave him a blow job. But it was an act of intimacy and tenderness that he didn't want to insert into this interaction with the white boy. He held onto the leather seat cushion as he exploded down Ben's throat. Ben choked a little, struggling to breathe again, but swallowed.

They avoided each other's eyes as Ben drove back to YouthRight to drop Raheed off a block away from the center so that people wouldn't see them together after hours. Ben didn't realize he was holding his breath until Raheed got out of the car. They arrived right before curfew, so Raheed wouldn't get in trouble. They would have to be more discreet next time. *Would there be a next time?* Ben asked himself. He could lose his position at the center and get kicked out of school. He was sure that Raheed was only a couple of years younger than him, so he couldn't get into legal trouble. Still, he could get into plenty of trouble with this father.

The thought of Raheed's dick in his mouth pushed out all other thoughts and his own hard dick reminded him of how much he enjoyed the evening himself. He could barely wait to get to his room at his frat house. He pushed past a bunch of brothers having an impromptu party and ran up to his room. Once he had locked the door, he laid on the bed and quickly shed his pants. He closed his eyes and thought of the taste and smell of Raheed's dick. How heavy it felt in his hands, how smooth it felt on his lips. Ben remembered the salty taste of Raheed's pre-cum and how heavy he was breathing. He thought about what it might feel like to have something so heavy and thick inside his ass, how it would fill him up. Ben came all over his sheets just as there was a knock on the door.

"Go away!" He yelled at the intruder, but when he heard his girlfriend, Misty's voice, he quickly put on his underwear and opened the door. Misty was wearing a floral jumper and saltwater sandals. He saw that she noticed the cum on the sheets, and she looked around for another person. "I've been thinking about you," he told her.

Raheed ran all the way back to the sitting room where the residents watched TV at night. The others were watching a horror movie on Netflix. Raheed did not like horror, but he didn't want to slink back to his room like he was guilty of something.

"Where were you?" One of the guys on the couch asked over his shoulder.

"I went to see my aunt." Everyone seemed satisfied with his answer. Throughout the film, all he could think of was whether or not the others could tell he let a guy suck his dick. *Did that mean he had sex with a man? Wasn't it official only if you let some dude fuck you?* He didn't know and it worried him. He kicked himself for not thinking of these questions before. But who would he ask? He didn't know any gay dudes, except D' Shawn and he seemed to be unsure if he was gay. Did it mean he was gay if he liked it? He decided right then that he didn't really like it and that he would never do it again, but it didn't answer the question of what if he was gay now. He decided to do a test. He left the movie early and went to bed before his roommate came in. Pulling up a porn clip from the internet on his phone, he masturbated thinking of the softness of the woman's breasts on the screen and the wetness of her pussy. After he came, he was satisfied that he was not gay and went to sleep.

Ben received a text that said, "You know who it is. Same time, same place tonight. Bring $."

Raheed met Ben in the same place where they had sex. "Young money. Father owns the Parker Foundation. Heir to the throne. I figure you been hiding out being gay from daddy a long time now."

"I told you I'm not gay. Where did you get my number?"

"Volunteer file."

"How did you know about my father?"

"Even street kids can use Google."

"Yeah, but there are a million Parkers."

"Not so many that have a DUI with a red convertible." Ben looked at him with a frown, but before he could speak, Raheed said, "Everybody's record is public, man. No secrets anymore."

Ben smiled. "Smart."

"You surprised, huh?"

"No, I mean—."

"You mean what? I bet all your life people thought you was smart. Rich equals smart. People never think you can be rich and dumb."

Ben laughed, thinking of all the people he knew who fell into that category.

Raheed felt nervous about the easy way they got along. He thought, *What could it mean if he liked him as a person?* He wanted to hate him. Raheed felt it was the key to feeling like he was using the white boy instead of the one being used. "Let's get this over with," he said, opening his pants.

An electric current went through Ben, making his body shake inside at the sound of Raheed unbuckling his belt. He hoped that his shaking wasn't noticeable. He wanted to maintain some level of cool dignity in this process and he feared it may already be too late for that. As he leaned across the front seat, Raheed stopped him.

"Wait. Let's go to the back. More room."

The two men stepped out of the car and into the backseat of the two-door car. Without the barrier of the divide between the front seats between them, it suddenly felt even more charged. Raheed immediately regretted his idea to move things to the back seat of the car. He felt himself start to grow before Ben touched him, and he closed his eyes so as to not see Ben's reaction in case he had a smirk on his face.

Ben was hopelessly rock hard and prayed that he would not cum in his pants. Raheed leaned back as much as he could in the cramped space. Ben leaned in. He moaned reflexively, both because of how much pleasure he had from being so close to Raheed and at the discomfort in his pants as he was straining against the fabric of his skinny jeans. He cursed the pants silently. Without thought, Ben unbuttoned his own pants. He reached inside his underwear and began to stroke himself. He could not stop his hand. He wanted to control himself and jack off after the encounter like he had the week before, but it was no use.

Raheed heard Ben's pants unbutton but decided to keep his eyes shut for fear that if he saw the white boy's stuff, he may push him off at the last minute and not collect his $100. He tilted his head back and tried to relax, which wasn't difficult given the pleasure he felt as Ben's warm mouth stroked him. Ben's breathing got quicker as he moved faster. Raheed felt his own breathing grow heavy and tried to stop himself from moaning, but the sound slipped out of him regardless. Raheed pushed Ben's head down, working himself deep into Ben's mouth and throat, not letting him breathe for several seconds. Raheed's hips began to move up and down and Ben kept up with him. The two moved in sync, building in intensity until Raheed managed to say, "I'm coming."

Ben choked a little less this time and swallowed, then what he could, and kissed and licked up what remained while Raheed shuddered at the touch of Ben's lips and tongue. Ben also felt himself rising to climax and came soon afterward. Ben and Raheed both pulled up their pants and straightened their shirts without looking at each other. Ben felt his face redden with shame. He remembered swearing to himself that he would never do this again. *How did this happen? He could have simply ignored the text message.* These were the thoughts that rushed to his head as he got back into the driver's seat.

Raheed, too came out of his post-orgasm fog with doubts about their arrangement. He realized that the hundred dollars he was getting was not enough. They traveled back to the center in silence. Raheed was lost in thought about what he could do to make more money. He already had a low-paying job at Jack in the Box. He did not want to meet-up with anyone else. One white boy was enough. The thought of older men made him cringe. He would have to think of another way.

"Thursday. Same time and place. Bring more money," he said to Ben. "This is going to cost you $150.00 next time."

Ben nodded, knowing that he would pay a lot more for the experience again.

The two men came back to the same spot every Thursday for three weeks. Ben spent the time in between the visits with Ben with Misty. He went to class, organized house meetings at his frat, and took Misty to dinner and parties. His life did not change much at all. He relaxed and enjoyed his Thursday nights with Raheed and the rest of his life with Misty. There were members of the house who were gay, but this felt different. They had boyfriends who also went to the same college. They went into the city and marched in gay pride. They had come out in junior high or high school. He had never looked at another man before Raheed. He wasn't attracted to other men. It was a private part of his life that he isolated from every other part of his life. He broke out into a sweat every time he thought about other people finding out. *So, they won't,* he thought. *I won't let that happen.*

Raheed was not making enough from their encounters, even with the increase to $150. Ben did not meet with him every week and school was more than the budget laid out in the college "how-to" guide. On the sixth encounter, Raheed hesitated before getting out of the front seat. He had been practicing in the mirror how to say this for days. But when the time came, he was too nervous to remember the way he practiced.

"Do you want me to, you know, do it to you?" Raheed's voice cracked a little as he asked. He could not manage to look into Ben's eyes while he waited for his answer, so he managed to look at the leather upholstery.

Ben sighed. A great burden had been lifted. He had been unable to get himself to say the words. He had been preparing for this for a couple of weeks. Ben had looked up the best ways to have a non-painful, pleasurable anal sex experience. He read articles and watched instructional videos on the internet. He looked things up in the middle of the night, afraid that his girlfriend and frat brothers would see him. He prepared himself each time he met with Raheed after the first time. He gave himself an enema before, hiding the lube, and condoms in a crevice in the trunk, with old rags on top of it in case Misty was looking around. He had a dildo he bought in a sex shop buried in his underwear drawer. He didn't want to risk it coming in the mail and having it opened by some well-meaning frat brother.

"$200," Raheed said as he made himself look into Ben's eyes. Ben nodded yes and the two climbed into the back of the car. Ben kept his shirt on but took his pants off all the way and laid them carefully on the front seat. Raheed just lowered his jeans and underwear to his knees. There was something about taking his pants all the way was too intimate and he didn't want Ben to get the wrong idea. *I just need the money,* he thought to himself.

The lube! Ben thought. He reached for his pants. "Sorry, I forgot the lube. It's in the back of the car."

"Don't worry, there is no one here. Just go get it."

"Right."

Ben ran out into the chilly night air. His heart was pounding. *This is going to hurt, but it will be OK.* He hoped so. He did not want his first time to be a failure. The thought made him tighten up. *Relax,* he told himself. *Just relax.* He dug through the trunk of his car and grabbed the lube, quickly moving into the back seat. He saw that Raheed was not looking at him. Did he change his mind? He closed the door and held Raheed in his hands, stroking him and bending down to put him in his mouth.

"Slow down," Raheed said, already hard. The two found the backseat of the convertible to be very challenging. They tried various positions but settled on Ben's knees on the seat with Raheed behind him, standing just outside the doorframe. Raheed was nervous. He watched some gay porn to help him get ready to fuck Ben, but he was still worried about hurting him and losing out on steady money. He had been having sex with girls since he was 14. *I know what to do,* he thought. He pushed in only to hear Ben cry out.

"Does it hurt?"

"Yeah. Slow down. Not so hard."

"Do you want me to stop?"

"No. Keep going."

"Does that feel OK?"

Ben managed a high-pitched, "Hmm." A sound he did not recognize coming from himself. He was trying to open up and let Raheed in but his body was burning from pain. He was grateful that Raheed was gentle and patient with him. He felt so vulnerable, so open, and with that thought, his body opened up a little. He realized that his vulnerability might be the key to getting through the night. He focused on Raheed's touch, the way he talked to him, his hand on his ass, the slow movements inside him.

"How does it feel?"

"Better."

Raheed felt the tightness of Ben's anus clamp around him. He pushed inside him, but it was difficult not to feel like he was hurting him. *This is not working,* he thought. He could barely get his head in without Ben flinching. What if Ben decided he didn't like it? What would happen to the extra money he needed? Raheed tried not to panic. He had always worked before. He tried to think of sexy things to say that might help but came up empty.

"Are you ok?" He whispered.

"Yeah. I'm fine." But Ben didn't sound fine.

"You feel good." The words slipped out of Raheed's mouth. Ben moaned in response, and Raheed was able to get a little deeper. "You feel real good."

"You're so big."

"You're so tight," Raheed said. As Ben opened more and Raheed began to lose himself in the feeling of being surrounded and pulled into him. Raheed could hear grunting noises and it surprised him that some of them were coming from him. "Oh, that's good. That's it." He heard himself say. For a moment, he forgot he was fucking a man and just enjoyed the grip on his dick.

They were both tired and didn't want to go anywhere. Ben put the top down and they sat together in the front seat, staring into the trees and sky. The sounds of small birds, planes flying overhead, and distant traffic filled the car. Neither of them had noticed before. Ben turned to Raheed and broke their silence.

"Why are you at YouthRight?"

"What, you wanna get to know me now? After all this time?"

"I see you all the time at work and I don't know anything about you really."

"Why, do you suddenly got questions?"

"I don't know. I don't want...I want us to at least be able to have a conversation."

Raheed rolled his eyes. "There's nothing you can't just find out from my file anytime you want."

"I don't want to find out from your file. I want to ask you. You can ask me anything."

"Who says I want to know anything about you?" Raheed laughed. He was serious, but Ben took his laughter for teasing.

"Come on, Raheed," he prodded. "How long have you been in Youth-Right?"

"Fine. A little over a year. My parents died when I was 14. Car accident. I was playing with my cousins and not in the car. The police showed up at my aunt's door and said they died."

"I'm so sorry, man. That's awful."

"Well, everyone at the center's got a story. At least I spent 14 years with my folks. At least they didn't throw me away or hurt me. They were good people."

"Why didn't you stay with your aunt?"

"I did, for a little while. She had four other kids and no room. My aunt's great, you know. That's my mom's sister. She's the only family I got left," Raheed said and turned away. "My dad was an only child, and my grandparents died a long time ago. I went to a couple of foster homes, but nobody wants a teenager to live with them. Especially, a Black teenager. So, when a bed became available at YouthRight, I took it. That's it. That's the whole story."

"My mom died," Ben said. Raheed turned to face him.

"Oh yeah? How?"

"Leukemia. She was only 40. She was beautiful, my mom."

"Did your dad remarry?"

"Yes. His best friend's wife."

"For real? Wow. At least he didn't marry some mail-order bride your age or something like that."

"It's still creepy. I've known her all my life. My parents used to travel together, have parties at each other's houses and everything. One day she's Aunt Barb and the next she's my new mom."

"Were they having an affair the whole time?"

"That's my guess."

"What did your dad's friend have to say about all of this?"

"Nothing. He disappeared. I see his updates on Facebook sometimes. He lived in Canada for a while, then Europe, maybe. I think my dad paid him to go away. That's my dad. Never met a problem he couldn't make disappear."

Gregory came to him after the house meeting. After the house meeting was a time of comradery and bonding—a party just for the members. Business and pleasure. Ben started drinking before he got to the meeting. He had a few beers in his room. He poured a rum and coke from the bar and sat down in the back of the living room. They droned on about house maintenance, pledge recruitment, and house finances. He saw Gregory looking at him and smiled back. Gregory pledged a year before he did but had to take a year off from school over getting caught with some drugs. When Gregory came back, he came to live at the house. Ben could feel the rum spread warmth throughout his body, lifting him up and away from the noise. There was nothing else but Greg and the rum. The members moved to the pool room, spilling over into the hall and up the stairs. Ben staked a claim in the chair in the corner. The pool room softened through his eyes. The brothers' voices receded into the background. Raheed was on his mind. He closed his eyes. He saw Raheed's brown eyes and long lashes. The curve of his face, the smoothness of his skin. He was so impressed on how smooth Raheed could get his face with a shave. In his mind Ben ran his lips over Raheed's cheek, carefully kissing his temples and eyes and cheeks, chin, up to his full lips. They looked so soft. Softer than Misty's lips. A series of thoughts ran through his mind. He would offer to pay him extra next time. *How much for a kiss? $50? $100? I can't pay for it. Raheed has to want to kiss me. It's ok,* he thought, pushing back tears. *That's not what he wants. I'm not what he wants. Maybe I should stop seeing him.* The idea made him want Raheed to be there even more. He would be OK with him just sitting next to him, looking at him with those brown eyes and long lashes. He felt a hand on his shoulder.

Greg was looking down at him with a fresh cup of rum and coke. "Hey brother, you look like you could use this," he said, handing Ben a red and white plastic up. "What's up?"

Ben looked at Gregory from his head down and back up. He was wearing a black T-shirt and black jeans. His blonde hair contrasted with the black. He had strong features, trim and muscular. Cute. He stood up and took the cup from Gregory's hand. "Nothing's wrong, now."

"Now?"

"Yeah. You're making it better. Thanks for the rum."

"My pleasure." He smiled and looked directly into Ben's eyes. Their brothers and friends swirled around them, playing beer pong, laughing, and even wrestling in the corner.

Ben ran his fingers through his hair. "Come with me," he said to Gregory. He led Gregory up to his room and closed the door.

"I don't think I've ever been in here before."

"Well, there's always a first time." He grabbed Gregory by the shirt. And grinned.

"Whoa! You got me up here, now what?"

He looked away, all of his bravery gone. "Will you kiss me?"

"Is that what's going on?"

"Never mind. Just go back downstairs and tell the others that I molested you or whatever," he said, falling back on the bed.

"Hey, hey. Shh. It's ok," Gregory followed him on the bed until he was on top of him. Ben put his hand on the back of Gregory's head and pulled him down into a kiss. Ben felt Gregory's body sink into his. It felt so good to kiss him. He allowed his imagination to wander to Raheed. He imagined Raheed's lips on his, Raheed's hands exploring his body, pulling off his shirt, kissing his neck and chest.

Ben kicked off his shoes and slid off his pants while Gregory also shed his clothes. Gregory kissed him, slowly moving down his chest to his stomach until he was kissing around his dick and on his thigh. Raheed's mouth had never been that close to his dick. He thought of Raheed's lips on his dick. He almost came just from the image. He grabbed his dick in one hand and guided into Gregory's mouth. Gregory went to work, pumping and sucking. "That feels so good," Ben said, as he arched his back and his body stiffened. One more stroke and he would be ready to cum.

"Not yet," he heard Gregory's voice from below. When Ben went to touch himself, Gregory moved his hand away. Ben groaned in frustration. Gregory slid up his body to kiss him more. Ben wrapped his legs around him. As much as Ben appreciated the kisses, he writhed in anticipation that Gregory would enter him.

"Blow me a little first," Gregory said. Ben hungrily and easily swallowed Gregory's dick down his throat. He tried to push back his disappointment. Gregory didn't have as large a dick as Raheed, but he was thick. When he felt he had worked hard enough he said, "Now, please."

Gregory immediately turned him over on his stomach. Ben reached over in his dresser for the condoms and lube. Ben pushed his ass up in anticipation as Gregory put on the condom. He felt Gregory's finger slip inside his asshole with lube, getting him ready. He closed his eyes and gasped when Gregory finally pushed inside him. "Yes," he said. "Right there. That's so good." He meant it, but it wasn't as true as he would have liked it to be. He wanted Raheed. *Not now,* he thought. *Stay with what's going on now.* He pushed Raheed out of his mind and concentrated on what was happening. Ben enjoyed Gregory's weight on him, the feel of his breath on the back of his neck, and the soft way he kissed his shoulders. He reached underneath himself to find his shaft. He felt Gregory deep inside him, tapping his prostate, making him want to explode from the inside out. He felt Gregory tighten up and then pull out. Confused, he turned around, "What's the matter?"

"Now, you do me."

"Huh?"

"Do me."

"I'm close. Give me a few more strokes."

"Here." Gregory handed him a condom and a bottle of lube.

"OK." Ben sat up and put on the condom. He was already losing his erection and had to concentrate to keep from going soft. He was surprised by how nervous he was. Ben had wondered what it was like to be inside of another man. Was it the same as with a woman? He realized he was so enjoying being entered and moved around, releasing himself to another person, that he didn't pursue topping someone else. This was his chance. He began to get hard again.

"On your knees," Ben directed, Gregory bent over and put his forehead on the pillow. Ben put on more lube than was necessary because he was afraid of hurting him. He teased Gregory's asshole until he heard him moan, and then he pushed his lube-slicked dick into him. His asshole formed a tight ring around Ben's dick. "Hmmm," Ben hummed. He didn't want to hurt Gregory, but his body wanted to push harder and faster. He went a little faster and found Gregory happily moaning underneath him. He increased force a little more with each push until he realized he was pounding into him, and Gregory was loving it. He felt Gregory tighten, spasming up and down his dick. He held on for a few more thrusts, and he, let go and came, finally. Being inside him felt good, tight, and warm. He missed being the one couched into orgasm, either with slow strokes or the fast beating he just gave to Gregory, who was already asleep beside him. *Probably had more to drink than I did,* Ben thought as Gregory turned over and nestled onto Ben's shoulder.

The next morning, Ben woke up to find Gregory still glued to his side. They were both naked and sticky from their first night together. Gregory's watch alarm went off and he stumbled out of bed, half asleep, to get to his first class, but didn't forget to kiss Ben on the cheek before he went. *Was this what it was like to be gay?* he wondered. Up until that point, he did not think of himself as gay. He didn't think of what he did with Raheed as changing his identity. They never spent the night together, never kissed, never took the time to touch each other. After being with Gregory, he realized he wanted those things from a man. And he wanted that man to be Raheed. "I'm so pathetic," he said out loud as he stared at the ceiling.

The first time Ben saw it, he thought he was imagining things. He prayed that he was imagining things between Kendra and Raheed. Kendra smiled at Raheed. Ben was taking the smaller kids out to the playground to play kickball, when he saw it. Kendra, with a circle of her friends, looking at Raheed and Raheed looking back. He had seen Raheed with girls before. They were always buzzing around him, trying to get him to notice them. Raheed slept with them once and then parted ways. This looked like it had been going on more than once. How had he missed it? Out of the corner of his eye, he could see Raheed and some of the other guys on the court with Kendra and her friends laughing and joking. Whenever Raheed scored, he looked at Kendra. Ben even thought that he saw him wink at her, but it was too far away to tell absolutely.

While Ben was paying attention to Raheed and his new girl-friend, a fight broke out on the kickball field that he had to stop. The other volunteer counselor was already there, trying to break it up and yelling for his attention.

"Damn, Ben! What the hell were you doing? You left me all alone with those kids. Not cool, man."

"My bad. I'm sorry," he said. Raheed's game was over, and all the older residents were out of sight. He wondered if he was fuck-ing her right then. *Where were they doing it? In the music room, where the other boys took their conquests? Or did he find somewhere special for her?* She was pretty. But not the prettiest in the place, that was for sure. She had a nice body if you like girls who were short and had a big butt. He tried not to hate her, but he couldn't help it. He imagined Raheed kissing her, holding her, touching her. It made him sour inside, like there was something wrong with him.

Sex with Gregory came easy. Ben suspected that the other mem-bers of the house knew but didn't say anything out of respect for their privacy. He thought about just making Gregory his only per-son like Gregory wanted him to be. But he always came away un-satisfied. Something was missing. Then there was Misty. Things had gotten so complicated. He spent time with her on the weekends and saw Raheed once a week and Gregory got what was left after studying and volunteering and house duties. Nothing made him feel like when he was with Raheed. He would stop seeing Gregory and Misty if Raheed said so.

They talked sometimes, mostly after their sessions. "I see you have a girlfriend now," Ben said.

"I guess so."

Raheed and Kendra hadn't talked about it, but maybe. He hadn't had a girlfriend for a year, just some sex in the rec room every once and a while. Then, he and Ben took up. Even though it had only been a few months, he was starting to think that the thing with Ben would keep him from ever having a girlfriend again. What girl would want him if she knew he was fucking some white guy?

"You never mentioned it, and I saw you two together yesterday."

"You're still watching me? I thought you got what you wanted."

"Everyone could see you. I didn't have to go looking for it."

"You're talking to me about having a girlfriend? What about you? Did you break up with whatever her name is? Not that you tell me anything. I'm just some hired dick."

"Hey. I just said that I saw you two. I'm the last one to tell you anything about who to sleep with. Let's just drop it," Ben said.

"You brought it up."

"I'm sorry. I'll take you back," he said, turning over the engine. They drove in silence. "Next week?" Ben asked.

"Sure. It's all about what you want, right?"

Raheed kissed Kendra more. Touched her more tenderly. He put her on his lap in the middle of the common room where everyone could see. *Was it just to get at Ben? Make him squirm since he told him he was watching?*

Ben waited for Kendra outside her apartment building. She had graduated from high school and lived with her mother, father, and brother in a two-bedroom apartment a few blocks away from the youth center.

"Hi, Kendra."

"Hi." She was shocked to see Ben leaning against his convertible.

"I'm Ben, one of the volunteer counselors with the younger kids."

"I know who you are. Look, I'm on my way to work."

"Say, you've been hanging out at YouthRight for a few months now, right?"

"Yeah, so? What do you want?"

"I also saw that you want to be an artist."

Ben kept his body language open and as non-threatening as he could. He didn't want her to get scared. He just wanted to talk.

"You looking up my file? What the fuck?"

"I'm just interested in helping the people that are part of the program. That's what I'm there for."

"Look, I don't date white dudes."

"I'm not asking for a date."

"You got a point, then?"

"I know of an art school in DC that has a one-year program in Baltimore for aspiring artists. You get a place to stay in a dorm, a work studio that you share with other students, special workshops with established artists, and a stipend. You won't have to work cleaning offices anymore."

He had her attention. "How do you know about this?"

"I know some people."

"I can't afford anything like that."

"I'll pay."

"What? Why?"

"Does it matter?"

"You're shitting me? Nobody offers something like that without wanting something in return."

"Not really. I'm just an altruist. Don't look a gift horse in the mouth."

"What in the hell is that supposed to mean? When is this all happening anyway?"

"This Spring, two weeks from now. Pack whatever you need, I will make sure your transportation is covered."

"Two weeks? I didn't even apply."

"I pulled some strings. Besides, I heard your art is amazing. All you need to do is send them a few pictures and it's done. Here is the email," Ben replied.

Ben gave her the number to the program and the email address of the director.

Kendra paused and looked Ben in the eyes. "It's Raheed, isn't it?" she asked.

"I don't know what you mean." Ben was not prepared for her to confront him about Raheed. He would rather she think he was some do-gooder.

"Everybody knows you're sweating him. Do you think you're hiding it?"

"Are you going to the school or what?"

"I'm going but fuck you," Kendra said and walked away.

Raheed found a note in his room asking him to meet Kendra in the parking lot. Raheed had to be on the property during certain hours and it was the only place still on YouthRight grounds that had some privacy. They stood out in the cold in a far corner of the parking lot where not a lot of people wandered. Kendra showed him the information from the art school Ben gave her. She said she called them, and he was telling the truth. She put in her application and if she got in, she was going to go.

"Did he try to have sex with you for this?"

"No way. He only has eyes for you."

"What did he tell you?" Raheed's heart was pounding. "What did he say, exactly?"

"He didn't have to say anything. I can tell how much he likes you. Look, everybody knows anyway. We can see how he looks at you."

Raheed tried not to betray the fear that flooded his body. He felt like running away. He didn't want Kendra to look at him. *They all knew. They would look at him differently.* He felt dizzy. He didn't know what to say.

"You can stop hiding. I'm not mad. A lot of people are bisexual. My cousin—"

"I'm not bisexual! I'm not gay!"

"OK. Calm down."

He just wanted to change the topic. Deflect to her behavior. "So Kendra, you sold out, took the money?"

"What, you're not going to take that white boy's money?"

Raheed looked away.

"So, you already have? I'm glad we used condoms," Kendra laughed.

"I told you I'm not gay!" Raheed was yelling, but not at Kendra. He was really angry with himself. He was nothing but a prostitute and Kendra knew it.

"Don't get in my face like that." She pushed him in the chest. "I'm not judging you. You're not the only one who has a family. Has dreams. I need this. Yeah, I'm taking the money. I guess you know what you're doing with that white boy or whatever, just be careful, OK?" With that, she touched his cheek and left.

Raheed was pacing up and down D'Shawn's living room. Although his apartment was a modest one-bedroom overlooking the river, D'Shawn was very proud of it. There were furry white rugs on shiny black linoleum floors and a built-in bar with stools. Real African art on the walls. He was even more proud that he knew where all the art was from. He knew what each mask was for and even what the contemporary art symbolized. His furniture was simple. A metal-framed leather sofa and chairs, glass tables with metal in-lay. Minimalist lamps. It was a million times better than anything he had ever seen growing up and just what he dreamed he could have but knew was out of his reach as a kid. His state-of-the-art sound equipment filled the apartment with R&B he thought would soothe Raheed.

"He bought her way into some art program," he informed D'Shawn.

"Now everybody knows what we're doing."

"Forget them. They are going nowhere fast and you know it. Did you love that girl?" D'Shawn asked.

"No, I guess not, but that's not the point."

"The point is that he's willing to do a lot to keep you."

"To own me."

"Don't look at it like that. Look at it like a business opportunity. He will pay real money. Not just $100 or $200 here and there. He's going to want to keep you close. Get more. $500. He'll pay more frequently. Maybe your own apartment so he can have you when he wants. You could really live well, save some spending money. Ask to go with him places. He'll pay. He wants the boyfriend experience. Look, I know this game intimately."

"I'm not like you, ok? I'm not going to let him just keep me like a favorite pet."

"Fuck you. You want to work at Shit-in-the-Box forever? What's your big plan after YouthRight kicks you out? Rent a room somewhere? Sell some drugs? Don't you already have a record? Next time they try you as an adult. Say you stay in school. How are you going to pay tuition at the community college and your rent at the same time? What then? How will you pay for a four-year college? Think, man. This is your shot. Take it."

"I'm not some kept boy. I'll make my own way."

He found a sober living house that he could move into. Raheed didn't drink or use drugs, but he got busted for selling pot a few years earlier, so he was able to get into the space based on his record. It was mostly for guys who were out on parole and looking for a permanent situation, but his counselor at YouthRight got him in. The house itself was an old two-story home that the landlord rented out through a deal with the city. There were three bedrooms that had two men in each one. The house had 1 bathroom upstairs and another half-bath on the first floor. There was a kitchen that they all shared, a living room, a small dining room, and a small bedroom where the house manager stayed that looked like it was probably a pantry or storage space at one time. The house manager, Timothy, lived there rent-free in exchange for keeping things orderly and free from criminal activity.

To Raheed, everything looked like it was second-hand from a homeless or youth shelter. There wasn't any trash anywhere, but the space showed wear on it from so many people coming in and out of the house. The living room couch and chairs had a ridiculous flower pattern that was worn thin with holes in some places. There was an old desktop computer in the corner that Timothy assured him was slow but worked. The coffee table and end tables were put together from different sets. Each one had scratches where previous residents had carved their names or other symbols. There was a large screen TV on a media console that had missing or broken shelves. The cable box was held up by two cinder blocks with a piece of wood between them. The carpeting was a coffee brown that still looked stained but vacuumed. The kitchen had basic appliances that had seen better days, but it was clean, and all the dishes were put away and the linoleum floor was recently mopped, even though there were visible cigarette holes and torn-up pieces. Keeping things running smoothly meant that Timothy had to put down strict rules. Raheed found out on his first day that no drugs or alcohol were allowed on the property. If he came in drunk or high, he was out.

Raheed was nervous but hopeful. *This was the right decision,* he told himself. He could no longer stay at YouthRight and he didn't want to wind up as somebody's plaything like D'Shawn. Timothy showed him to his room, which was really just one-half of a tiny room next to the bathroom that he shared with the rest of the house. He had a twin bed, a nightstand, and two drawers in a dresser. Pretty much the same things he had at YouthRight, except their rooms were bigger. There was old carpeting in the room that was worn bare in spots. The room was so small that the door bumped into the dresser when they opened it. His roommate wasn't there. Timothy informed him that his roommate worked at an Amazon warehouse as a sorter and had different hours every week. Raheed didn't have much in the way of things, just a duffle bag of clothes and a backpack for his books. He put his clothes in the drawers he was assigned and took out his books.

It was the first week of classes for the Spring term and he didn't want to fall behind. He went downstairs to the living room to work on the house computer. It took a while to warm up, but it finally came on.

"I bookmarked the best porn sites if that's what you're looking for," said a tall Latino guy walking in the front door.

"Naw. I'm just doing homework."

"I'm just kidding. My name is Hector."

"Raheed."

"Good to meet you. Well. Don't let me stop you. School is important. Keep working."

Hector turned around to face three other guys who were making their way up the front steps.

"This is George, Mateo, and Donell. Guys, this is our newbie, Raheed." The men filed in and waved at Raheed.

"You all work together?"

"Yeah. We work construction. Right now, we are putting up a high-rise downtown. We're about to have dinner. You want some? It's your lucky night, I'm cooking." The men sat in the living room with potato chips and soda and turned on the TV while Hector went inside and started to bang on pots and pans. It was impossible to study. Raheed couldn't tell them to be quiet and there was no other computer to use. He decided to just relax for a while and talk to his new housemates. He watched a vampire movie and ate homemade hamburgers with them until they went to bed. The house was quiet by 10 and he went back to the computer to work. He was falling asleep but managed to stay awake until the computer crashed at midnight and he didn't have anyone to ask what to do.

Raheed went back to his room and found his roommate already asleep. He must have come in when everyone else was talking or eating. He missed YouthRight already. They had several donated state-of-the-art computers and printers in a designated study space that was monitored so people didn't go in there to fool around. There was a small library and it was just a couple of bus stops away from school and walking distance from work. Now, he had to take two buses to get to school and work. He took off his clothes and got underneath the covers. *It's all going to be worth it,* he told himself. Then, he heard his roommate snore. It was soft at first and then grew louder as he tossed and turned. He closed his eyes and put the pillow over his head. He thought about what D'Shawn said about getting Ben to give him more money. He did the math in his head and figured that he would have to spend a lot more time with Ben to get his own apartment. He asked himself how far was he willing to go.

Raheed got back into the front passenger seat of Ben's car after one of their sessions. "Drop me off at the library at my school. I have to use the computer."

"I have a computer in my room. You can use it." Raheed's look told him that his offer came off as an excuse to have more sex. "I won't even be there. I've got to meet a group for class," he added. Ben handed Raheed the keys to his room off his keychain. "Just put these on the table in the hall when you're done."

"Won't your brothers think I'm there to rob them?"

"They're not racist! People's friends come by all the time. I'll text them ahead of time if it makes you feel better." Raheed rolled his eyes at Ben's trust in his frat brothers but took the keys.

Raheed took a deep breath before he walked into the frat house. It was cleaner than he expected. There were men and women scattered around studying, playing pool and video games. People noticed him when he walked in, but no one said anything. He went up to the only nonwhite person he could see and said, "Ben said I could go to his room and study." A dark-skinned Latino guy directed him to the room on the top floor. It was much bigger than any bedroom he'd ever seen. Ben had a private bathroom, his own television and gaming setup, a computer, and a printer. He even had a large window with a window seat. It was much easier to study and write on a computer with fast internet service and using a working printer. When he thanked him the next day, Ben offered his room for their next time together. Raheed thought it was too intimate, but he also liked using Ben's equipment, so he agreed.

Raheed rolled over in exhaustion. His all-nighter caught up with him. He fought sleep. Ben reached over him to pull out a joint and lighter from his nightstand. He closed his eyes at the feel of their chests touching through their T-shirts. Another second and he would be hard again. "Have some before you go." Raheed took the first hit. They lay side by side, blowing smoke up at the ceiling.

Raheed felt it immediately. "Whoa. This is good shit, man. Where did you get it?

"I got a guy."

"Well, he's got the hookup." He paused for a second and looked at Ben. "I bet you've gone out with a lot of guys."

Ben giggled. "I totally wanted you to think so. I was so nervous the first time! I never touched another man before you."

"Really? Not even in high school."

"Nope. The closest was Mr. Hobbs. He was my sex-ed teacher in

8th grade. When he talked about sex, he used the official language. 'The penis enters the vagina and ejaculates...' But when he said it, I don't know, I got a hard-on."

They both laughed. "Was he real handsome or something?"

"To me he was. I mean, he was a nerd that wore knock off sneakers and a bow tie every day. At first, he wore slacks and then he switched to suspenders with jeans. One night, I dreamt I was in class and that it was just the two of us in the room. He was at his desk, and I was walking over to him and before I could get there I came. I woke up with it all over my pajamas. Dwayne Hobbs," Ben sighed.

"Dwayne Hobbs?" Raheed laughed so hard he bent over slightly and clapped his hands.

"What's so funny?"

"He's Black, isn't he?"

"So? How did you know?"

"Dwayne? Come on."

"I still think it's just a coincidence."

"You think you and I are a coincidence? You don't see any connection there?"

"I was twelve. Like I said, he was the only one. I'm done. What about you?"

"I don't have a Mr. Hobbs in my life. All girls."

"C'mon. Nobody you even looked up to?"

"There was this one guy, Gary."

"He must be white."

"Actually, he isn't. He was the son at the last foster home I was in. The whole family was nerdy and kinda weird, but I liked them. Gary was a senior and I was a sophomore. He was real smart. Like genius smart. I mean, he got into a bunch of colleges, and they were all begging him to take their fellowships. His parents were so proud. He used all kinds of big words and at first, I thought he was stuck up. Once I figured out he was just really nice, I started looking up the words he used. I would scribble them down somewhere, spelling them the best I could, and then I'd look them up after everyone was asleep. He helped me with my homework. He's the one who told me I could go into child advocacy law. He said I could help kids in the foster system. I was really into it. They were nice people.

"I messed things up, though. I hung around with some kids who said that they could hook me up with some easy money. It sounded like nothing. All I had to do was deliver a message. They didn't trust phones or paper because they could be brought into evidence. Everything else is hearsay. So, I went back and forth with messages I didn't understand. All I cared about was the tips. A joint and $20 here and there added up. I got some Jordan's and other stupid stuff. One day, the cops busted in. I was in the house. They said I didn't have to be dealing for them to prosecute me. I was there and I had a joint on me. Turns out they were major dudes. The feds were in on it, not just the city cops. That was it for me. I was facing 18 months in juvie. It was my first offense, so I got off with probation after a few months. But the family didn't want me back. They said they had other kids to think about and that I was a bad influence. I came to YouthRight straight out of juvie."

"What was juvie like?"

"Shitty." Raheed was annoyed with the question. "How did you think it was? I gotta go back to the house."

"Stay the night."

"You never stop, do you? You got to hear about the exotic life of people like me, so let's just leave it."

Ben looked hurt, like a puppy he had just bonked on the nose with a rolled-up newspaper, which made him even madder.

"I didn't mean to—"

"If I don't come home before 11, I lose my spot. Then where will I go?" Raheed quickly pulled up his pants and looked for his shoes. He thought, *if I don't leave, I'm going to beat the shit out of this white boy, and then what would happen?*

Ben looked away. A part of him wanted to say, "live with me," but another part wanted to keep his life as it was. It was simpler this way. Ben put on an old-school playlist in the car on the way back to the sober living house. "I like old school," he said.

"Oh yeah? That's cool. You got any D'Angelo?"

"You know it."

Raheed had to admit, he loved riding in the car. It was smooth and fast. The seats felt like sitting on a marshmallow. He had always wanted to ride in a convertible but figured it would be among the million other things he would not get to experience in his life. He let the air slide across his body and looked up at the stars. He could hear the sounds of the street, too: a woman yelling into her cell phone, two guys on a stoop with a stereo, and other cars' booming bass. Women on the street and in other cars noticed them and waved or smiled or checked them out.

One Black lady who looked like she was in her 40s pulled up next to them in a BMW and said, "Do you two come as a package?"

"It's just you and me, girl!" Raheed yelled as they sped off.

Raheed told D'Shawn about what happened the day before at Ben's frat house. "I was on my way up to Ben's room when I was faced by some blonde dude."

"So, how long have you known Ben?" Gregory stepped up to Raheed and stood close to his face.

Raheed didn't back away. "A while. Why you want to know?"

"I'm just his friend and want to make sure he's OK."

"OK? What do you think I'm going to do to him?"

"I'm not accusing you of anything. I'm just looking out for Ben."

"I think Ben can look out for himself. Why don't you tell me what this is really about."

Gregory took another step forward, putting him only a few inches away from Raheed. "Alright. I think you are a hustler, and you are using Ben for his money."

"Whoa, whoa boy, back up," said one of the frat brothers who came rushing through the door when he saw the two men. Raheed noticed a couple of the other brothers of the frat coming into the room to see what was going on.

"Why don't we all just calm down and back away," said the frat brother who was trying to keep the peace.

A tall guy who looked older than the rest of the brothers grabbed Gregory by the arm. "Come on, Gregory," he said. "Let it go."

Gregory threw up his palms. "There's nothing to let go. We are good so long as you know your place."

"Know my place? You want to go white boy? I'm right here." Then three other people came between, separating the two of them. "Get up off me," Raheed said, pushing them away.

"Gregory could be a problem," D'Shawn told him.

"I know."

"You are going to have to kick it up a notch."

"What does that mean?"

"I'm not sure. See where things take you."

Ben was laying on his bed reading while Raheed was at the desk with his own textbooks and his back to him. "I met your boy Gregory when I came to get my things the other day," he said over his shoulder.

"Oh yeah?"

"Yeah. He seems pretty protective of you."

"You could say that."

"You slept with him or something?"

"Yes," Ben said.

Raheed turned toward him.

Ben got up and sat on the edge of the bed. He looked serious. "So?"

"You're going out with him now?"

"No."

"He sure seems to think you are."

"I don't care what he thinks."

"How many times did you sleep with him?"

"A few. Why do you care?"

"I don't."

Ben shrugged. "OK, then," he said and laid on the bed again, facing the wall, trying to read, but the words ran together.

Raheed turned back to his books.

"At least he kisses me," Ben said as he turned back toward Raheed. Raheed did not move. Ben picked up another one of his books from beside the bed and started to read. He didn't want Raheed to leave. He looked at Raheed's shoulders and saw the tension in them. "Don't worry about Gregory. Let me rub your shoulders," he told him.

Raheed knew it was an intimate gesture and tensed against the feel of Ben's hands.

"Come on, it doesn't mean anything. You've been inside me, but I can't massage your shoulders? I promise to be good."

Raheed relaxed a little and sat back in the chair, letting Ben touch him. *It's like getting a massage at a spa*, Raheed told himself. Ben's hands were firm and probing. When he relaxed, it started to feel good.

"A little to the left," Raheed said.

"Over here?"

"Further."

"Now?"

"Yeah."

"Breathe deeply. That's what a masseuse told me once."

Raheen let himself breathe into the fingers touching him. He relaxed his shoulders and let his neck and head drop slightly in the front to maximize the relief. He felt himself touch Ben's right hand and tried not to think about why.

"You want me to stop?"

Raheed guided him around to the front. He grabbed Ben's chin and pulled him towards his lips, then slid his right arm around Ben's waist. For the first time, he kissed him. Raheed pushed away questions in his mind about why and what it meant, and just did it because he wanted to. *So this is what it feels like to kiss another man, he thought.* Raheed pulled away for a moment. "I just wanted to know what it felt like," he said. "You know…"

Ben touched his forehead to Raheed's and slid his hands to Raheed's shoulders. "Me too," he said. "Can I feel it again?" Ben asked, quickly moving in to kiss him before he could say no. Ben paused to take off his T-shirt. He took a chance and began to pull off Raheed's shirt as well, hoping that he wouldn't stop him.

Raheed allowed Ben to take off his T-shirt, touch his bare chest, slide his hands on his abdomen, and slowly kiss his lips, then his neck. Raheed gave in to what felt good. *Fuck it,* he thought. *Why not?* Ben reached to touch himself. Raheed pulled Ben's gym shorts and underwear down to his ankles. Raheed noticed that it was the first time he saw Ben completely undressed. When felt the air around him on his bare torso Raheed became aware of his own nakedness and almost pushed Ben away. He watched Ben kneel before him, kissing his chest and abs. He made his way down his front while Raheed lifted his hips off the chair, allowing Ben to pull off his shorts completely off.

Ben kissed Raheed slowly, savoring every minute. He removed Raheed's shoes and did the same for himself. He moved to the bed and laid down on his stomach. Raheed walked over and turned Ben on his back swiftly, landing between Ben's legs, causing him to catch his breath. Ben had never been on his back before, and it made him feel even more vulnerable. He could see that Raheed was searching for something in his eyes. Affirmation? Love? Ben winced at the idea that Raheed could see his need for something else between them. He did not like being so exposed.

For the first time, Raheed took Ben in his mouth. The feeling of another man's dick in his mouth was not as unfamiliar as he thought it would be. He felt in control. He smiled to himself, I *always thought I was the one in control.* Ben lifted his hips to meet Raheed's mouth. Raheed worked Ben's dick with his tongue, licking his shaft and then playfully circling his head. He made his way up his body to kiss Ben on the lips again. He reached over to the dresser where Ben kept his lube and glided it across himself and Ben. He decided that he liked the look on Ben's face as he pushed into him. It was a combination of pain and pleasure. Facing Ben that way made him want to kiss him. It enhanced his pleasure and Ben looked immersed in his own.

Ben bit his lip not to make noise, but still made whimpering sounds that he feared could be heard in the hall every time Raheed pushed into him. Raheed's sounds were soft and rhythmic as he beat against him harder. It did not take Ben long to come. Raheed began to pull out when Ben stopped him. "Keep going," he said. Raheed was surprised that Ben came again a few minutes later. By the third time Ben looked like he was going to come, it was too much for Raheed and he finished inside him.

The two men lay side by side, still feeling the aftershocks of their orgasms. Ben was afraid to say anything to spoil the moment. He closed his eyes and indulged in romantic fantasies. Whenever Raheed had sex with him, he imagined scenes of the two of them holding hands at dinner, walking in the snow, and sharing a hot tub. He smiled to himself at how silly he had become, but he liked these fantasies. They made being physically close to him more like being emotionally close. This time, Raheed was curled around him. He felt his arm across his chest and his breath against his neck. Nothing had ever felt so good.

Raheed pretended to be asleep, but he was thinking about Gregory. It had not occurred to him that someone like Gregory could replace him. He felt stupid. *Of course, Ben could find someone else like himself.* He thought it would be another Black man, desperate, in need of cash. Or maybe the girlfriend would demand more of his time. The Gregory thing threw him off and made him feel he wasn't enough for Ben. "Did you like sleeping with him?" Raheed asked, suddenly coming alive.

"Who, Gregory?"

"Are there others?"

Ben liked this new interest in his love life. *A little jealousy was never a bad thing,* he thought. He rolled over to sit up on his elbow, facing Raheed. "It was OK."

"Just, OK?"

"First of all, he wasn't as good as you. Second, he insisted I do him every time."

"And you weren't down for that?"

"You know what I like."

Raheed laughed. "Yeah, I guess."

Ben ran his hand over Raheed's chest and abdomen. He felt the smoothness of his skin and ran his fingers over the outline of his tattoos. There was a male lion on his chest and a lightning bolt on his left arm.

"Why a lion?"

"I just like them. They don't let anyone take anything from them. They rule their territory."

"I wish I had tattoos," Ben said. "If I were to get one, which one should I get?"

"I don't know, maybe one of those Celtic symbols with the three prongs or something."

Ben looked at him with surprise.

"Man, you are constantly surprised that I know things." Raheed shook his head. "Stop looking at me like that."

"I know. I just didn't think they had those in your...neighborhood."

"Yeah, well, we have a lot of things in my neighborhood you don't know about." Raheed sat up and looked for his underwear.

"I'm sorry. I always ruin things, huh?"

Now he's whiny, Raheed thought. "I just have to finish studying for this exam," he said.

"Do it here."

"Too many distractions here," he smiled even though he was annoyed.

Ben smiled too. "OK. See you soon?"

"Next Thursday."

Ben handed Raheed money. "I can't next week. Maybe the week after? Let's text about it."

Raheed gathered all of his things and made his way to the door. He tried not to show his frustration. This was the third time Ben put off their meeting. Ben lifted his head like he was hoping for a goodbye kiss, but Raheed wasn't in the mood.

"I put something for you in your backpack," Ben said. Raheed nodded. He waited until he was on the bus to look inside his bag. It made him feel less like a prostitute to not check the amount in the room. He found $500 cash and a $200 gift card. The card would come in handy buying books and food. The $500 went into his apartment fund. He almost had enough for a deposit on a room in a house and a few months' rent. He thought, *If I do this right, I could leave my trash job at Jack in the Box and have a place to stay. But what if I can't get him to have more meetings? Everything is too uncertain,* he thought, biting his nails, a habit he started when he started this thing with Ben. *What do I even call this?* That question had been on his mind for the past few weeks. He didn't think it was a relationship. Yet, they were more than just friends. It made him crazy to think that Ben was calling all the shots.

Ben and Raheed could hear a woman's yelling in the hall.

"Where is he?" Ben was shocked to hear his girlfriend, Misty's voice in the hall. With all the excitement of Raheed and Gregory, he all but forgot about Misty. She pushed her way into the room. Both men were sitting in their underwear on the bed.

"What the fuck! Really? Right in your room where we have sex? Why didn't you tell me you were gay? I had to hear it from my friends! Did you have to sneak around behind my back?"

"I'm not gay," Ben said.

"Well, you look pretty gay right now from here!"

"You look pretty gay from here, too," Raheed said, putting on his gym shorts. Ben shot him an angry look.

Ben tried to make Misty understand as he slid off the bed, reaching for his jeans." I wanted to explain things, but there never seemed to be a good time—"

"You know what? Fuck you and him and this whole house of fucked up losers."

A group of people had gathered outside the door and stared into Ben's bedroom, taking in the drama. Misty pushed her way back down the stairs.

Raheed laughed to himself. *Now Ben knew what it felt like for all his friends to know his business in public.* He shook his head as Ben stood in the doorway, not knowing what to do next.

Raheed was about to leave as well. "No. Stay. Please," Ben begged.

"It's time for me to go. Find your girl. Talk to her," Raheed said.

He made his way past the silently gawking frat brothers that lined the walls. He wondered why they acted so surprised. Hadn't they heard them in the room? Ben was especially loud. Gregory seemed to know what was going on.

For Raheed's nineteenth birthday, D'Shawn invited them on a weekend trip to the lake house of one of his clients.

"I want to lay eyes on this white boy you've been talking about so much," said D'Shawn.

D'Shawn's client, a white man named Dave, was pale, doughy, smelled vaguely of stale cheese and looked to Raheed like he was in his 50s. He treated D'Shawn like his property, touching him constantly, and demanding that he sit on his lap even when D'Shawn seemed uncomfortable. Everything about him was repulsive to Raheed, but he didn't ask D'Shawn why he put up with him. He assumed by the size of the lake house and its elegance that D'Shawn was being paid a lot to deal with this guy. Ben chipped in for what he called "incidentals"—maid service, private boat rentals with a captain, and a private chef.

Dave and Ben were sunbathing on the deck while D'Shawn and Raheed went swimming.

"D'Shawn told me you and your boy have a similar arrangement that he and I do," Dave said.

"I don't know what you're talking about."

Ben's suspicions were right! He heard of men having secret affairs with their secretaries or prostitutes even, taking them on expensive trips. He was sure his father did it both before and after his mother's death. He never knew anyone with a young black man in tow. He thought Raheed and him were the only ones. But he assured himself, they were in a relationship and the part of paying him was just to help Raheed get on his feet after YouthRight. Ben didn't know what else to say, so he put on his sunglasses and tried not to look guilty or surprised.

"You're young, though," Dave said. "I would think you could get it for free. But, as they say, there's no free lunch. Right?"

Ben smiled but didn't say anything. Were they really like Dave and D'Shawn? No. He had real feelings for Raheed. *But did Raheed have real feelings for him? Raheed and I are different. We have a relationship,* he thought. He lounged back in his beach chair, enjoying the sun.

"Did you tell your, 'I contribute to the marriage equals one-man and one-woman campaign,' dad about this relationship?" Ben turned toward him. He said nothing, but wondered if this guy was a business associate of his father.

"Look, kid..."

"I'm not a kid."

Dave chuckled. "OK, Ben, we all want a taste of something different. Something to piss off the parents or blow off steam, but don't get this mixed up with real life."

"I think I'll take a nap." Ben got up from the lounge chair with doubt ringing through his head.

"Suit yourself. But don't say I didn't warn you!" Dave called after him. *What if this guy told his father for some blackmail scheme?* He seemed like he would stoop that low. His father would surely disown him. Was this worth it? He watched Raheed enjoying the water with D'Shawn. Their wet, dark bodies shimmering in the sun. *What if this was wrong?* He wasn't so naïve as to think that Raheed would be with him if he didn't have money. *But was there nothing genuine between them?* He saw Dave running down to the shore waving and joined the two in the water, splashing.

The private chef was named Charlotte. She was a white woman in her late 30s with brown hair and an average face and body. She walked around in a bikini and Raheed noticed her breasts as she moved. He tried to hide his interest, but she saw him checking her out. She smiled. Charlotte brought her own herb garden, hanging it on the door in the pantry on what looked to Raheed like a shoe rack, but had smaller white pockets. She made foods that Raheed never heard of. The first night for dinner, they had Thai coconut soup, pappardelle with salmon and peas in cream sauce, ending with a banana cake with cream cheese frosting. Raheed didn't love it, but he didn't hate it either. Ben seemed distant since they went swimming, and he knew he would have to work to elevate Ben's mood if he wanted to have a decent time himself. *This is a hard job,* Raheed thought. He wondered if he was getting paid enough for all the work that he put into keeping Ben happy. The thought made him resentful of Ben's neediness.

They went to bed and Raheed reached for Ben's dick despite his anger. He knew sex was part of the arrangement in exchange for the fancy lake house and private cook. Ben redirected Raheed's hand to his chest. "I think we should just sleep tonight." Raheed turned over, relieved. They heard D'Shawn's moans down the hall. *D'Shawn sounded like he liked it enough,* Ben thought, *but was he thinking of someone else the whole time?* D'Shawn's moans got louder.

The two men were lying with their backs to each other. "Are you asleep?" Raheed asked.

"With all that noise?"

"Yeah, I know."

"Raheed? Do you think what we're doing is wrong?"

"What do you mean?"

Ben turned to face Raheed. He reached out to touch him but pulled his hand back. I mean, "Dave told me that he's paying D'Shawn to be with him. I'm not stupid. I know we have an arrangement, but is that the only reason you're here?"

Raheed's heart raced. What should he say? What would D'Shawn tell him to say? He turned over to face Ben. He was sick of having to babysit this white boy's feelings all the time.

"I'm here because I want to be," he said. Ben traced the line of Raheed's face with his finger. Raheed could tell that Ben didn't believe him. He didn't believe it himself. Would he be there if it also meant that he couldn't be at a fancy lake house? He had to say something, but he had to get it right. It had to be sincere and intimate. If he didn't, he could blow the whole thing. Forget the extra money and saving for a place of his own. He cupped Ben's face in his hands and looked him in the eye.

"Tomorrow, we are going to go to the graves of my parents and there is no one else I'd like to be there with me," Raheed said, touching his forehead to his. He meant it. He didn't have any friends left besides Ben, D'Shawn, and maybe Timothy.

Ben smiled and pulled Raheed to him for a kiss. D'Shawn and Dave were finally quiet. "I think we can sleep now," he said to Raheed and he put his head on his shoulder. Ben's body relaxed and Raheed closed his eyes, hoping that he got it right.

Raheed woke up right before dawn and found that he couldn't sleep. His mind was racing with thoughts of money and sex and the fact that he was going to his parent's graves. *What would they think of him? Would they be ashamed?* He never heard his parents say anything homophobic, but he was sure they would not want their only son to be a hustler. They would be disappointed in him.

He went to the kitchen in his boxer shorts to get something to eat and found the chef cutting up fruit and arranging the food for the day's menu.

"Wow, you're early," she remarked.

"I couldn't sleep."

She was wearing an oversized T-shirt that just covered her ass.

She was skinny with a small ass that was not like the thick round bodies of Black women Raheed was used to, but he wondered what was underneath her T-shirt anyway.

"Neither could I," he said.

"Open your mouth and close your eyes," she said. He complied and she put a strawberry with fresh cream in his mouth. He opened his eyes to find her standing very close to him.

"That was good," he said.

She reached up to kiss him and he leaned into the kiss. She let his hands explore her body. He felt underneath her T-shirt and found that she was not wearing underwear. She moved to the counter and bent over, resting her arms on its cool surface and spreading her legs slightly. Raheed was surprised. Nothing quite like this had ever happened to him before.

"I don't have any condoms on me," he said.

"It's OK," she whispered. He was stiff with anticipation of her wetness. He pulled himself out of his shorts and crouched down to meet her waiting body. He held her small breasts with one hand and the counter with the other as he pushed into her. Raheed was grateful to be inside a pussy again. He had not had sex with a woman in months. Between keeping Ben happy, school, and his job at Jack in the Box, he didn't have time to pursue women. Ben was his full-time job, and Jack in the Box was a side hustle. As he fucked Charlotte, he worried that Ben would wake up and find them and all his hard work would be for nothing. Charlotte seemed to be enjoying their time. She tried to keep quiet but kept letting out little moans. He finished quickly, putting himself back in his shorts. He managed to say, "Thanks," and kiss her on the cheek before running into the shower to wash off before Ben woke up.

He slipped back into bed and put his arm around Ben, who snuggled up next to him. *How could I be so stupid?* He berated himself. *What if Ben woke up or Dave heard us?* This could all be for nothing.

"You're up early," Ben stirred next to him.

"Yeah. I wanted to see the sunrise," he lied. Raheed spent the rest of the time at the lake house trying to avoid the chef. They didn't talk, but he could tell she was disappointed in his performance.

Ben and D'Shawn went with him to his parents' gravesite. He cried almost as hard as he did when he first got the news of their deaths. He didn't think about if they would be ashamed of him; he only thought how much he missed them. He also felt a wave of anger. *I wouldn't have to be hustling like this if they had just kept their asses home and not gotten into the car,* he thought. Both D'Shawn and Ben tried to console him, but he didn't want to be touched. When it was time to go, he heaved a sigh and thought, *Well, back to work.*

Ben rode on top of him. The rhythm of his body rocked Raheed gently. He was vaguely aware that his eyes were half-closed and his mouth slightly open. He breathed in rhythm to Ben's movements. Ben had his hands on Raheed's chest and his eyes closed. Raheed was lost in the sensation of tightness and the stroke of Ben's body moving up and down. The pressure to come had been building for some time. He was close. The rocking and the sweet way Ben's body felt on top of him, put him over the edge until it felt like he was flying on his own mounting pleasure.

And then he said it. "I love you." Just like that. Raheed released what he was holding back and came, pumping into Ben. With his head back and his eyes closed, he exhaled into the softness of the bed. Then he opened his eyes. Ben was staring at him with a look that was full of hope and fear at the same time.

"Do you mean it?" Ben said, shifting to being on Raheed's side.

I said it! Raheed thought. He didn't know why he said it right then. *Why did I say it doesn't matter? What do I do now? I will have to call D'Shawn as soon as I leave.* The two had talked about it before. Raheed was afraid that it would come up and he would not know what to do, or worse, that it wouldn't come up at all and he would be out of favor.

"Look," said D'Shawn, "you stay in control of the 'I love you' bomb. It's important not to do it too soon, or he'll get suspicious and run scared. Too late, and he will be even more suspicious and get pissed."

"So, when do I do it?" he asked.

"That's the art of the game," D'Shawn smiled.

Raheed left their time together even more confused and thought for the millionth time that he was in over his head. Now that he had said it and Ben was looking to him for confirmation with such anticipation, Raheed knew he had to commit to it.

"Yes, I mean it," he said, pulling Ben in for a kiss. He smiled at Ben, but inside his mind was racing. *What have I done?*

Ben's mother's sister died suddenly from a heart attack. The moment after he got the call, he contacted Raheed. After work, Raheed sat with Ben while his friends and frat brothers came by his room to offer condolences. Gregory looked beside himself with anger and jealousy. Raheed tried to ignore him, but he couldn't help but relish in his misery.

"The funeral is on Saturday. Do you have a black suit that you can wear?" Ben asked.

With that question, Raheed realized that he had become the serious boyfriend, not just the guy you call to fuck. He felt uncomfortable in the role and thought he wasn't ready to take this step or sure that he should, but he was trapped by telling Ben that he loved him, at least for a while. It was now a relationship. He realized that he was beginning not to know the difference between his true feelings and the ones he showed to keep the game going. *After the funeral,* he thought. *I have to make it clear to him that I'm not his boyfriend.*

When they arrived at the family estate, Raheed felt the weight of being the poor Black gay boyfriend in a sea of rich white people. The family drama was intensified by the recent loss. Ben, his father, stepmother, sister, and brother barely spoke to each other. Everyone looked at Raheed like he was lost. Ben insisted on holding his hand, which made Raheed sweat with discomfort. The only person to welcome them was Ben's sister, Melanie. She looked like a slightly older, female version of Ben. She shook Raheed's hand. "My brother knows how to make an entrance," she said, smiling. Raheed was grateful for her. She stayed by them through the service.

At the reception, Ben's father finally addresses his presence. "Who in the hell is this?"

"This is Raheed."

"You've got to be kidding me."

Sensing a big scene about to unfold, Raheed tried to pull Ben away. The rest of the people at the reception moved closer to see the fight. Raheed saw the giddy anticipation in their eyes. It made him sick.

"I've been trying to call you for weeks." Ben's voice was shaking.

"If this is what you were going to tell me, I'm glad I didn't fucking answer."

"I don't know why I try with you—"

"Shut up," Ben's father interrupted him. "Raheed, is it? Come with me." Raheed followed Mr. Parker into a smaller room, where he closed the door. Raheed imagined that there were a bunch of people with their ears to the door. "Ben may be naïve, but I'm not. I've known about your little affair for some time now."

Raheed looked confused and shocked. "How...?"

"Ah. I've got my eyes and ears everywhere," Ben's father said, pleased with himself. "His little ditzy girlfriend went running to her father, who happens to be a friend of mine. I know you're some kid off the street that he picked up while he was volunteering. Dumb fuck. I told him to concentrate on getting into business school and be careful where he unzipped his pants. I knew he was an idiot. I thought it was going to be some girl he knocked up. But I never imagined you. Listen, stay away from my son. You've had your fun. Probably milked him for some money. Let go while you still got a little something out of it. Play it smart, and don't wait around for him to dump you for one of his own kind when he's through slumming it."

Raheed was taken aback. He didn't expect Ben's father to be so blunt. He fought back tears and took a deep breath to keep his voice from cracking. Most of all, he was hot with rage. He looked the old man in the eye, "Your son came after me. He insisted I come here. I don't want to be here. Tell him to keep his hands to himself." Raheed stormed out of the room.

He heard Mr. Parker yell, "I'll do just that!" behind him as he walked directly to the parking lot. He hoped that Ben was behind him so he wouldn't have to call an Uber to get out of the fancy club where they had the reception.

Ben came running up behind him. "Let's go. I'm sorry you had to go through that." They got into his convertible and drove back to the city. Ben spent the drive complaining about how terrible his family was. Raheed tried to breathe and tune him out.

"I'll pay your tuition at State. The tuition is not that much."

Raheed restrained himself, looking at Ben with less contempt than he felt.

"I mean, tuition is within my budget. If you get in, I can pay for it."

Raheed swallowed the anger and shame he felt and tried to focus on the opportunity. He always wanted to go to State. It wasn't a large city. The university students made up a big chunk of the town. He had seen those students all his life but didn't think it was possible to join them. He knew that Ben was just rebelling against his father, but why not take advantage of it?

He sat in front of Ben's computer, trying to finish a homework assignment. Mr. Parker's words rang through his head, "Let go while you still got a little something out of it." *What did he get exactly? A few hundred dollars?* He was almost able to get out of that damned sober living house and get his own apartment. He couldn't afford his own computer. He realized that they had been at this for almost a year. He applied to four-year colleges, but where was he going to get the money without Ben? Going to college, having a career was his parents' dream for him. *Can I really pass up the chance to go to college, just because I don't want to owe this white boy anything? Was this all just a waste of time?* Ben was sleeping peacefully after having been fucked.

When in a playful mood, Ben sometimes got on his knees and asked him, "How can I service you?" He said it staring hungrily at Raheed's dick. At first, Raheed kind of liked the idea of being attended to and pleasured on command. As he sat in Ben's dorm room, which was bigger than the living room of the house he lived in, he felt angry and used. Ben rested while Raheed sat up and worried. *This isn't working,* he thought, *but can I afford to give it up?*

"How much do you need this week?"

"Do you think I like asking you for money?" Raheed's frustration and resentment tumbled out of him.

"I didn't mean anything by it." Ben was caught off guard, wondering what he said wrong.

"I finished my application to the university. With Pell grants and loans, I can get by. I'm almost done saving to rent a room."

"What are you saying?"

"I don't know." *I want to end this. I'm tired of working for you,* Raheed thought, but instead asked, "Don't you have a class?"

Raheed hadn't asked him for more money than they agreed to, but Ben knew he needed it. He put everything he had in the room, $800, in the front pocket of Raheed's backpack when he wasn't looking. Ben hoped that Raheed would find the money and realize that he was willing to take care of him.

Ben asked Raheed to wait for him downstairs while he put together his clothes for the day and gathered his books. Ever since the confrontation with Greg, Raheed hated to be alone in the frat house. He felt that the other brothers were always watching to make sure he didn't steal anything, even the Black ones. He went to the bathroom on the first floor but left his bag on the couch so that everyone knew he wasn't sneaking around. When he came out of the bathroom, he heard the police politely knock at the front door. Raheed instinctively became anxious when he saw them but tried not to worry, or at least to not show how much they shook him. He had never seen cops so well-behaved. He figured they were there to talk to someone about their missing bike or something. There were two white cops, a short one with curly brown hair and a big red-headed guy who looked like he could have been a professional wrestler before he was a cop. Raheed stayed far away and prayed that Ben come down soon so he could get away from the cops and the house.

He overheard their conversation. *I guess cops talk loud everywhere they go,* he thought. "Someone placed an anonymous tip about drugs being sold from this location." Raheed's blood ran cold even though he didn't have any drugs and didn't take any, he knew that it wouldn't matter because of his record.

Gregory was the first to speak up. "Good morning, officers. Everyone here is a member of the house, except for that man in the living room. I've seen him using in here, but no one has bought from him that I know of."

Raheed stood up. Both cops surrounded him.

"Why don't you calm down. What do you have in the bag?"

"You are going to search me, just because he said so?" He was trying to keep his anger in check, but he was seething with rage.

The cop with the curly hair slammed him against the fireplace. The one with the red hair barked at him, "I ask the questions. You seem squirrely to me. Like you've got something to hide."

"I don't have anything to hide and nothing in the bag but books," Raheed struggled to talk with his face against the mantle.

"Is this your bag?" asked the cop with the red hair. Raheed rolled his eyes. The cop pulled out a baggie with pills and a wad of cash. Raheed's heart sank. There was nothing he could say that would convince the cops that he had never seen those things before. He knew that the truth had no place in his immediate future.

As the police handcuffed Raheed, all the frat brothers gathered around, whispering. Gregory had a big grin on his face. Ben came running down the stairs. "What's going on?" He looked around frantically for someone to give him an answer. He went up to the cop with the curly hair, "This is my guest and I demand that someone tell me what's happening!" The cop ignored him. Ben got a basic sense of the story from his frat brothers. "What! Drugs? He didn't have any drugs 10 minutes ago." Ben ran over to the arresting officers. "Please, listen to me. He didn't have any drugs."

"Step out of the way. This doesn't concern you," he said. And they were gone.

Ben looked around at his frat brothers. "All this was happening and you just let them take him? No one came to get me? No one stood up for him?"

"I don't like to see another Black man arrested, but face it, they found the drugs and the cash on him. He's guilty," one of the Black members of the house said.

"What? I just gave him that money a few minutes ago and there were no drugs in his bag."

The rest of the members of the house looked away and talked amongst themselves or left for class. Ben was left exasperated and alone in the living room. Gregory was nowhere to be found.

It took several calls to find out where they took Raheed. Ben tried explaining things to the cops. He was certain that they would let Raheed go once he told them that the drugs weren't in his bag and that he gave him the money. He could not find the arresting officers, so he talked to another cop. This one was about 20 years older than the cops he saw at his frat house. His manner was calm, but Ben could tell that he wasn't really taking him seriously.

"So, you see, officer, Raheed could not have had the drugs before. He must have been set up," he explained, trying to keep his voice from cracking.

"Look, Brian, is it?"

"Ben."

"Ben. I'm sure you want to stick up for your friend..."

"I'm telling you the truth."

"Why did you give him so much money?"

After a pause, the older cop read Ben's expression and talked before he could respond. "He's your boyfriend? Does he frequently ask you for money?"

"He didn't ask me for anything," said, offended. Ben told the cop that he wanted to surprise Raheed with the cash and how much Raheed wanted to go to State, but he was already flipping through the other files on his desk.

"So, why don't you go home and we will take it from here."

"Can I see him at least?" Ben asked.

"You have to register as a visitor two days in advance. They can give you information at the front desk. And let me say, you should get yourself a better class of boyfriend."

Ben was Raheed's one phone call. He tried to contain his panic so that the other inmates didn't think him vulnerable. "Your little boyfriend, Gregory, set me up. I didn't have any drugs or money."

"I know. I put the money in your bag as a gift. There were no drugs in there."

"Can't you tell these people that?"

"I tried. They don't believe me. I'm going to get you out of this."

"It looks like you got me in this in the first place."

"Do you know what you're charged with? They won't tell me anything."

"The cops wanted to know about Oxi being sold on campus. Some white kid overdosed. They asked me about a whole bunch of people I never heard of. If you don't do something, they are going to pin all the drugs on campus and that kid's death on me."

"What? They can't do that!"

Raheed hung up on him. He didn't want to ever hear Ben's voice again.

Raheed didn't see that much difference between the county jail and the juvenile facility he was in years ago. He was in a cell with 3 other inmates. One was an old dude about 50, the others were around his age. All of them were Black. There was some blood and vomit in the middle of the floor. He wondered what they did to someone that made him bleed that much and then throw up. Or was it the other way around?

He called out through the bars to the guards, "Hey, can we get some cleaning supplies over here? A rag or something? Looks like someone threw up in here!"

In response, he heard a couple of guards laugh. The other inmates looked at him like he was stupid for trying. It was a lot like juvie.

After he called out to the guards, Old Dude came up to him with a friendly smile. "Hey, young blood. You need anything? I can make sure you get soap, food, shoes. Anything you want."

Raheed knew what would happen if he took so much as a bar of soap from anyone. He realized at that moment that he was not successful in hiding his panic. Old Dude sniffed him out as young and afraid. "Nah, I'm good. Thanks," he said with all the calm he could muster. Inside, he was shaking so badly that he felt like he could fly apart at any moment.

A couple of days later, D'Shawn came to visit him in jail. Raheed was so angry, it was hard to feel happy to see him.

"You alright?"

"I'm OK. I don't deserve this man."

"I know. Ben is working to get you out."

"Fuck him. I should have never hooked up with him. What was I thinking? I'm not like you."

"What's that supposed to mean?"

"Don't be offended. I mean, you was always like this. All the kids talked about it. You're used to this."

D'Shawn looked like he was about to cry. "You was always good at school, Raheed, but this is real life. This is the calculus test right here. How much are you worth versus what you actually get back from life." D'Shawn shook his head, "Fuck all them that said shit behind my back, to my face, to my moms. I did what I had to do. We didn't starve and we didn't get kicked out." D'Shawn paused, "And fuck you for thinking you're better than me."

Raheed didn't know what to say. He watched his only real friend walk out of the visitors' room. He was alone.

Ben was at Raheed's arraignment. He found out what Raheed was facing. The judge didn't look up as he read the charges. "Raheed James, you are charged with aggravated trafficking of drugs and resisting arrest."

His court-appointed attorney was a thin, balding white guy in his late thirties who had the wearied demeanor of someone who was ready to retire. He explained that Raheed faced up to 5 years in prison because he had prior arrests for drug possession and petty theft as a minor. The judge set his bail high, $350,000, with ten percent down using a $35,000 bond.

"I don't want your drug dealer friends bailing you out," the judge said.

The attorney said he had three other clients being arraigned in the same courtroom. "I can plead you down to 2 years."

"Hell no! I didn't do it."

The attorney shrugged and entered a plea of not guilty, but never asked Raheed what happened. By the time the judge hit his gavel, the lawyer was already walking over to his next client on the list.

Ben felt helpless. Raheed didn't look at him when they took him away. Seeing Raheed in handcuffs broke Ben's heart. *This is all my fault,* he thought. Guilt ate away at Ben. He had to get Raheed out of jail, but his bail was more money than Ben had access to. *There is only one place to go.*

When he showed up at his father's office, he knew by the smug smile on his father's face that he knew what the visit was about.

"Your boyfriend got arrested! I tried to warn you."

Ben didn't ask how his father knew about Raheed. He assumed that his father was having the whole family followed. *Paranoid asshole,* he thought. "Raheed didn't have any drugs."

"I knew you were naive, but I didn't think you were this stupid," his father huffed.

Ben expected insults. His father had been calling him stupid and worse all his life. This time, it made him angry. "You want to know how the drugs got in Raheed's bag? The other guy I fuck got jealous and planted the drugs in his bag to have me all to himself."

Ben was surprised at his words, but not more than his father. The smile was wiped from his father's face.

"You have the nerve to talk like that to me, boy?"

Ben did not want to pursue the conversation any further. Better to get the money and go. "I need $35,00 to pay Raheed's bail. Like I said, it was my fault he's in this situation. I'm not asking you for money, I just want access to my trust fund."

"All of it is my money. You're not getting shit to bail out your drug-dealing hustler boyfriend." Ben realized there was no persuading his father. He turned to leave so he wouldn't see him cry. He knew from experience that a sign of weakness would only make things worse.

"If you have to be gay, son, do you have to defile yourself with someone like that?" His father said before he reached the door. He could hear his father's voice crack a little. He'd only heard him sound like that when his mother died. Ben left without turning around.

In the car, he allowed himself to cry. "OK. Stop crying and think," he said to himself. *Think, think, think.* Then, it occurred to him—Uncle Jackson. Uncle Jackson was a colleague of his father's and an old friend of his mother. She used to meet him for lunch sometimes. Ben once asked her if she was having an affair with him. She just laughed.

"Ben, come in. It's been too long. You've grown into a fine young man." Uncle Jackson was gorgeous. Tall, dark-skinned, poured into his Armani suit. He didn't remember him as sexy. Ben was getting a hard-on and had to force himself to concentrate on the issue of Raheed's bail. He told Uncle Jackson all of it. Paying Raheed for sex, the money he left in his bag, the jealous frat brother—everything. He didn't care what he thought about him, he just wanted him to help Raheed.

To his surprise, Uncle Jackson calmly listened without judgment. He was quiet for a moment and then he said, "Do you know why your mother and I were such good friends?" Ben shook his head. "Because she supported me when I was about to make partner and the others wanted to fire me for being Black and gay. She was the one who forced your father to make the other partners back down."

Ben was stunned and very proud of his mother. He missed her even more.

"I'll do you better than giving you money. I'm going to put you in contact with a friend of mine who's an excellent defense attorney. He'll take your friend's case pro bono."

Raheed was shocked at how quickly things turned once he had a fancy attorney. The brother was young and well-dressed. Raheed was impressed with how he walked into their meeting already knowing a lot of the details of his case.

"I read the complaint. It seems they ignored key evidence from a witness who said you didn't have any money or drugs before being arrested."

"Yeah. You talked to Ben?"

"He and I spoke on the phone. Look, I'm not going to sugarcoat this. You have a juvenile record, but it's minimal and you tested clean. What you've got going for you is that your record is clear since you came out of juvie. I can get this down to probation, but I don't think they will believe that it wasn't yours."

"It wasn't—"

"I know. Ben told me about the jealous lover. The court won't care unless that guy confesses. They want to tie you to the other drug traffic on campus, but they have no evidence. Witnesses contradict the cops resisting arrest claims. I can get that dropped. You can walk out of here tomorrow. If you stay out of trouble, this can go away with misdemeanor possession."

Raheed knew he should have been grateful, but he was furious. He didn't do it, be he was going to have to pay anyway. "Thanks," he managed to say through his rage.

"I'll give you some more free advice. If you're going to hustle that white boy, get smarter or get out."

Raheed went back to his aunt's place. On the second night, he was woken up by laughter coming from the front of his aunt's house. He saw the crew of guys sitting around in his aunt's living room, eating Cheerios and playing video games with High Point semi-automatics on the coffee table, and knew his cousin was dealing out of the house.

"Aw man, Cuz! Are you kidding me? How long has this been going on, man?"

"You remember Big Jim?"

"Yeah."

"Well, he ain't with us no more and I am."

The other guys nodded and laughed in agreement. "You right, man. That's how it goes," they said.

"How come you don't do this at your house?"

"Too hot right now. Cops been snooping around."

"How long do you think it's going to take them to get here?" Raheed panicked. "I can't be around this," he said pacing between the couch and the kitchen. "You get busted, or my probation officer sees this, and I'm gone for good," he said. "No get out of jail free this time. I got to get out of here." He went through the house gathering up his things.

"Yo, cuz, what you doing? Stop running around and relax."

"Man," Raheed said to his cousin, "I wasn't here, OK? Don't give out my name or my number to nobody."

"Aw, Cuz, you paranoid? Don't be like this," he said, still concentrating on the game.

"No really, I'm out. You see any more of my stuff around?"

"You didn't have nothing but some books and what's in that backpack and shit."

Ben grabbed his backpack on the dining room table and his bag from the spare room. "Tell Auntie I'll let her know where I am when

I get settled."

"OK, man," he looked up from his video game. "No beef? We cool?"

"Yeah. We cool." The two shook hands.

Raheed went out the back door and ran down the street to the corner store. His heart was pounding and he was having trouble breathing. Instead of standing like he thought he was, he realized that he was leaning against the wall of the store. His head swirled. *Breathe. Breathe,* he told himself.

"Yo, brother, you OK?" A small group of men began to cluster around him.

"Yeah," he managed to say, "I'm fine, man. You don't have nothing else to do?"

"Hey, I'm just trying to do the right thing," the man said backing off. "You know, fuck you." The other men moved back but watched him.

Raheed closed his eyes to keep from crying. He knew he couldn't stay there much longer. Those guys saw him upset and were probably sizing him up to rob him. They may try to take what little he had. *Where am I supposed to go?* He couldn't go back to the shared housing program. They kicked him out of his room as soon as he got arrested. He screwed up his friendship with D'Shawn. If he didn't have a place to stay, he would be in violation of probation. He knew the answer. There was no other answer. He dialed the number.

"Raheed?"

He took another breath. "It's me."

"How are you? Are you OK?" Ben asked.

"I'm fine. Look..." he said, taking another breath. "Look, can I come over?"

"Of course. Anytime."

"Now, I mean."

"Do you need me to come get you?"

"I can take a bus."

"There are no buses out here this time of night. I'll come get you."

Raheed covered the phone with his hands for a moment and tried to think. *There is nothing else. Go on, do it,* he thought to himself. "OK," he said to Ben. "I'll be at that 24-hour sandwich place near my campus in an hour."

Ben thought of asking why he couldn't go get him where he was but thought better of it. His mind was racing, trying to figure out what Raheed's call meant. *Was he not angry anymore? Were they back together? Was he in trouble?*

Raheed got on the bus to the community college campus. It was a twenty minute ride, and he wanted to collect himself before talking to Ben. His breathing still wasn't completely right, and he had to process what he was agreeing to. Raheed sat in the sandwich shop watching the students go in and out with their sodas and greasy bags of fries and thought about what was ahead. Near Ben's campus there were all kinds of different restaurants and shops, but at the community college, it was the sandwich shop or nothing. His duffle bag and backpack were on the table. *That's all I have in the world,* Raheed thought.

Ben pulled up in his red convertible and everyone in the store and on the street stopped. He tried to walk calmly into the store, but he rushed in fueled by worry. He saw Raheed sitting by himself with his bags. "Are you OK?" he asked, reaching for Raheed's hands, but he pulled away. Ben felt a sting in his heart but stayed focused on helping.

All was quiet in the restaurant, which had been full of noise and life just a few minutes earlier. Raheed looked around at the people staring at them. "Let's not talk here," he said to Ben.

"Sure. I'll take you anywhere you want to go."

They got in the car. Raheed felt uncomfortable with the memories he had of the backseat of that car. When he started this, he thought he was using Ben. He laughed now at that idea.

"Where to?"

"Just drive anywhere."

"What's going on? You have your stuff. Where are you going?"

Raheed stared straight ahead, trying to find the words. "You know how you asked me to move in with you after I got out of jail? Will you still let me? I understand if..."

"Yes. Yes, of course. You need a place to stay?"

"Just for a little while."

"Stay as long as you want."

"I won't need it forever," Raheed said, with some attitude. "I can pay rent until I find a place." This was not true, but he wanted it to be.

"OK. I didn't mean...I'm sorry. Just, whatever you need."

"I got some conditions. Things can't go back to the way they were."

Ben swallowed. They weren't getting back together, he wanted to be friends. *It'll be fine,* he said in his head.

"I'm not a hired dick. I have other things about me, you know. We are not doing that kind of thing anymore, alright?"

"Of course," Ben said quietly, watching the road.

"You know, we can be friends."

Ben was dreading that word. "Yes, friends. Of course," he said.

Raheed heard the sadness in Ben's voice. He felt the guilt rise in him. "If anybody should be mad, it's me. It was great to have the lawyer and all, but I was going along fine and if it wasn't for your friends, your ex-boyfriend, none of this shit would have happened."

Ben was determined not to cry. "You're right. I'm not arguing with you."

The fact that Ben was in agreement with him made Raheed feel even more guilty. "Look, I'm not trying to hurt you or nothing."

"I get it. Friends. I have a boyfriend now, anyway. His name is Brad."

"Brad? He's white?"

"No. He's African American."

Raheed laughed. *You will never change,* he thought.

"There are Black people named Brad!"

"I bet his mama calls him Bradley. She probably didn't want people to know he was Black just by looking at his name," Raheed said.

The two rode the rest of the way in silence looking straight in front of them. The city streets slowly faded and were replaced by nice homes and townhouses. They pulled up to one of the only apartment buildings in the neighborhood. Raheed knew from looking at the outside that the apartment was going to be nice. He was not disappointed. Ben opened the door to a two-bedroom apartment with vaulted ceilings and exposed beams. The kitchen was the whole wall of the right side bookended by the door and the first bedroom. There was not a wall to the kitchen. Instead, a sunken living room spread before a large window and balcony with a view of the city from the living room couch. On the balcony, there was a breakfast table and two chairs. The floor was polished dark wood. The couch and oversized chairs were white.

"This is it," Ben said. Raheed stood and took it all in. "My father is very generous."

Raheed nodded.

"This is your bedroom. Right now, it's an office, but it has a bed and I'll move the other stuff over against the wall tomorrow. There is a small bathroom next door and a full bath in my room. I'm sorry about that, we'll have to share."

Raheed put his things down on the foot of the bed. Compared to the rest of the place, it was plain. The room was outfitted with a small, flat-screen TV, a bed, and a dresser. He sat down, took a few deep breaths, and said to himself, "It's OK. I can do this."

Raheed threw himself into his schoolwork. He got into State before he was arrested. He missed the Fall term, but he insisted on starting in the Spring semester despite all that had happened. The school academic counselor suggested that he take the semester off and "get back on track." His aunt told him to work for the semester and then go back. He was eager to continue living the life he had started. With probation and getting out of jail, he started going to classes a week after the semester had already started. He registered late and had to take a bunch of courses he didn't want, like Physiology and British Literature, to fulfill his last requirements. Ben paid his tuition and bought a car so that he could drive himself to campus. *Just another thing he has over me.*

Raheed tossed and turned. He could hear Brad laughing in the next room. *Everything was about Brad these days,* he thought. *Ben and Brad. Brad and Ben. They say it like it's a thing.*

"It's not a thing," he mumbled under his breath. He couldn't do this without his friend. He needed D'Shawn.

Raheed got up the courage to call D'Shawn. "I'm sorry. You were right. I'm not better than you or anybody. You're a good friend and I'm sorry I hurt you."

"I'm glad you called."

"This Brad person is going to mess up your whole thing," D'Shawn said.

Raheed could feel him scheming from the other side of the line

"You've got to get rid of him. Does Ben like getting fucked by this guy?"

"I don't care what the two of them do," Raheed said. "I just don't want him to get me kicked out."

"Are you jealous?"

"Me? No way! It's always been strictly friends since I got back."

"You're a little jealous. That's good," D'Shawn said. "Use it as motivation."

Raheed didn't think twice about Ben asking him to lunch in the rich part of town. "There's this little café that I just think you are going to love," he said. Raheed shrugged and barely pretended to be interested. He knew that no one he grew up with would be caught in some hipster café, so he wasn't concerned about it. The moment they arrived, Raheed knew he should have asked more questions. At first, it looked like a regular café in white people's neighborhoods: real wooden tables and chairs, random couches, art on the wall. Raheed thought the menu was overpriced and full of crap only white people would eat. Avocado toast with sprouts started at $15 and you could add $2 if you wanted vegan cheese on top; $4 for extra veggies. He knew Ben was buying so he opted for the chicken and Black bean burrito, a smoothie, and some pie. He didn't wait to hear the total, but left Ben at the cash register to order something for himself while he found a table. When he sat down, putting the little metal stand with his order number in the middle of the table, that's when he looked around and truly understood where he was. Two men were kissing on the couch while another guy with a mustache, makeup, and hotpants talked loudly on his cell phone. Two women were eating lunch in the corner opposite their table; they sat on the same side of the table pouring over what looked like household bills, pausing to eat and whisper intensely to each other. Raheed was shocked. He had no idea there were gay cafes. Bars and clubs he knew about, but gay places where you could buy food in broad daylight were new to him.

"This place is great, huh?" Ben came bouncing up to the table. "One of my brothers in the house took me here the other day," he said placing his order number next to Raheed's. I thought you might like it.

Did he just tell me he's dating another man besides Brad? Raheed thought, taking in this information with some curiosity but decided to save his questions for later. "I didn't know places like this existed," he said truthfully.

"I know, right." Ben took off his jacket, looking around at the other patrons. Raheed and Ben sat for a while, making small talk. A few minutes later, the waitress stepped over to the table with part of Raheed's order.

"I'm sorry, we're still working on the smoothie," she said. From the moment she walked over, Raheed was hooked. She was beautiful—tall, smooth dark skin, big brown eyes, full lips, large breasts—she was mesmerizing. She walked away and he chided himself on not saying anything. What could he say in front of Ben?

"Uh, hello?" Ben said, waving his hand in front of Raheed's face. "You know I'm still here?"

"Look man, I'm just taking in the sights," Raheed said gesturing toward the waitress. "You knew I was straight when we started this thing."

Ben laughed.

"What's so fucking funny?" Raheed asked. Ben didn't have time to answer before his food arrived.

"Hey, sis, what's your name?" Raheed asked.

"Destiny," she said, smiling and flicking the name tag pinned to her apron. "What's your's, brah?"

"Raheed," he said. Before he could think of anything else to say, she was already walking away. "Where's my smoothie at?" he asked before she disappeared in the kitchen.

"It'll come out when it's ready," she said over her shoulder laughing. Raheed watched her ass as she walked away. He liked her.

"You know she's a transsexual," Ben said flatly and loud enough for other people to hear. Raheed couldn't see her, and he hoped that Destiny was not in earshot.

Raheed snapped out of his trance. "What do you mean?" he whispered.

"She was born a boy," Ben snapped. This was a mean side he hadn't seen in Ben. Raheed didn't like it.

He was going to ask Ben how he knew that but he changed his mind. He didn't want to hear whatever spiteful story Ben was going to tell and stopped Ben before he said anything else. "I don't know much about this world, but I know you probably weren't supposed to do that."

Ben shrugged. "Come on. Let's go."

"But I didn't get my smoothie."

"Please, the smoothie's here suck," Ben yelled, moving towards the door.

Raheed didn't see Destiny as he walked out the door. He came back to the café every day that week and he brought a single red rose with him each time.

Every day he asked, "Can I get your number?" She walked away each time he tried to talk to her. Finally, he put a message and his number and his number on a piece of paper that said, "I'm sorry about the other day. My friend is an asshole. If you ever just want to have a conversation, give me a call."

He was happily surprised when she texted him and asked if he wanted to come over for dinner. Destiny's apartment was small but clean. He liked the bright colors and butterfly motif. She had butterfly pictures on the walls and little butterflies all over the studio apartment. She put time into making a meal that smelled delicious. Raheed was hungry for time with a beautiful woman more than he wanted dinner. They didn't make it to the first course.

Raheed buried his face in the softness of her breasts. They felt so real. He didn't care if how she got them, he was grateful for them. Touching Destiny made him remember how much he liked women's bodies. He caressed her thighs and arms and belly, taking his time to savor the smoothness of her skin and the feel of her body. He could not imagine a universe where this person could have ever been called a boy.

He put a condom and lube on his dick and Destiny sat on his lap, leaning her back against his chest. She moved her ass in small circles, forcing a deep sigh from him. He guided his dick inside her. He held onto her breasts as she thrust him deeper and deeper inside her. After they were done, Raheed never wanted to leave.

Destiny led him out of her apartment so sweetly. He didn't realized that she had kicked him out until he was standing in the hall looking at her closed front door. He was hooked.

A white BMW with dark windows slid beside Raheed as he was walking back to Ben's place. The back window rolled down, but he kept walking. Raheed knew it could only be one person who would want to talk to him riding in a car like that.

A voice came from inside the car. "I have a proposal for you," Raheed recognized Ben's dad's voice. "It involves money," he said opening the back door.

Despite the small voice inside that told him to keep walking, Raheed stopped and got into the car.

"You want me out, isn't that right, Brad?" The tension between Raheed and Brad escalated from an argument about who was next to use the shower and spilled into the living room.

"Brad would never say anything like that," Ben said, coming to his defense.

"That's sweet. Taking his side already."

"There are no sides here. You can stay here as long as you need. I'm not forcing you out."

"But you want me gone, too."

"You're being paranoid."

"I have a reason to be paranoid, I'm about to lose my home."

Brad looked down at his shoes. "This place is a little cramped," Brad said. "You can't see what's in front of your face, Ben. You're so in love now."

Ben ignored him and went to Raheed, "Don't do this to yourself. We can come to an agreement."

"Agreement? I didn't agree to this. Did you finish slumming it like your dad said you would?"

"What do you mean?"

"After your aunt's funeral, your dad said this would happen. He said that you would get tired of me and go off with one of your own kind. I guess he thought you would trade out the Blackness. He was wrong, huh?"

"Don't listen to my father, but I'll make sure you are taken care of...."

Brad gave Ben an angry look.

"I see what's happening here," Raheed said, walking to the door. "You don't own me and you can't buy me off either. Good luck with this one. I know your dad will be happy. Tell 'em Brad."

"Raheed, don't go like this," Ben said. Raheed grabbed his jacket and slammed the door on his way out.

Damn, he thought, getting into his car. *Damn, damn, damn. This is exactly what I didn't want to happen. I should have played it smart, like D'Shawn said. Now what am I going to do?* He suddenly realized that it all could go away. Ben could decide to take back the car and stop paying tuition. "I'm back where I started," he said aloud. I have nothing. "Just as broke, with higher tuition payment." He remembered what it was like in his cell, alone and vulnerable to whatever that world would do to him. He started to cry. He couldn't cry then, but no one was around to see him cry now.

The words, "buy him off," stuck in Ben's head. He remembered what he did to that girl from the center. His dad wouldn't try to bribe Raheed to leave, would he? *That's what I would do,* Ben thought.

Ben could not get the last thing that Raheed said out of his mind. He did not want to be the kind of partner that spied like he had been before. He did not want to be like his dad, but he couldn't help but wonder what Raheed meant about being bought off. A couple of days after the incident, his thoughts got the better of him. *One look at Brad's phone is not a violation of his privacy,* he thought. He waited until Brad had unlocked his phone to text someone and left the phone in the room. It took him a few tries, but he timed a moment when Brad left the room and his phone's screen was still unlocked. Once Brad was gone, he went to the text archives and scrolled through them. He stopped when he saw his father's number. Brad had been smart enough not to use his name, but he was too trusting and did not erase their conversations.

That night, he and Brad were holding each other on the couch, watching a movie, but all Ben could think about was Raheed. *Where was he? Was he OK?*

"You're thinking about him, aren't you?" Brad asked. "I can tell you're distracted."

"I'm sorry, but he was so upset when he left," Ben said.

"He'll be fine. He just has to get used to the new situation."

Ben sat up to face Brad. "This is where he lives, you know. Without this, he has no place to stay."

"You've taken care of him long enough. You pay for his tuition, am I right?"

Ben didn't say anything.

"I knew it!" Brad stood up. "This guy is a little hustler who is taking advantage of your kindness."

"I owe him more than you can know."

"You're guilt can only go so far. It's none my business, but I bet he'll be fine without you."

"You're right. It is none of your business."

"If you want to, you can keep him like your favorite pet, but I thought we were building something here. The two of us, not the three of us."

Ben stood up to look Brad in the eye. "What did you call him?"

Brad yelled in frustration and threw a pillow across the room. "You're so in love with him, you can't see anything else."

"What do you mean 'he'll be fine without me'? Did you pay him to leave?"

"What? I'm not your dad."

"My dad? What's he got to do with anything?"

Brad walked away and Ben followed him, trying to pry out a confession. "Did you pay Raheed off to leave? Is that why he said he 'couldn't be bought?' Were you in on things with my father to get him out of my life?"

"You're so fucked up!"

"You didn't answer the question, what about my dad? Did he pay you to see me?"

"Why do you think the worst about your father all the time? It was nothing," Brad turned his back on Ben. "He approached me at the country club and just said you were single, and he thought we would be a good match, that's all."

"That's all? How come you didn't tell me about this? My dad told you to ask me out?"

"It's not like that. It was innocent. A father wanting his son to be happy."

Ben sat down and put his head in his hands. "I think we should take some time to figure out what our next steps are."

"You're dumping me? Your favorite Black toy went for a walk and now you are dumping me?"

"No, my boyfriend made a deal with my asshole of a father behind my back."

"You know, fuck you. Keep your toy, but you're not doing him any favors. He's right, you don't own him. I'll have someone come for my stuff."

As soon as Brad left, Ben went to Raheed's room. He didn't know what he was looking for exactly, but if Raheed was planning to leave because of a sudden windfall of cash, there was probably some evidence. Ben carefully went through Raheed's things, while keeping an ear out for his key in the door. He started with Raheed's desk and made his way through his clothing drawers. There it was. A check for $5,000 signed by Ben's father. It was dated two weeks before. Maybe it meant he wasn't going to cash it? Why keep it if he wasn't thinking about it? He put it back and waited for Raheed to return.

Raheed drove to Destiny's. "What's going on, baby?"

"He's kicking me out."

"Are you sure? That white boy would have kicked you once he got his new boyfriend if he wanted you out."

"Well, his guilt finally wore off because we had a talk tonight about me going somewhere else."

"Come here." She held him. "It's OK. Hey? You still have his father's check, right? You were saving it for a rainy day. Cash it and start a new life."

"You think so?"

"Maybe one here with me."

He kissed her and reveled in her softness. He took his time, he realized, for the first time in his life. Mostly sex was fast and hot, like he was burning a piece of paper. This time, he slowly undressed her, savoring the darkness of her skin, kissing her neck and arms. He had an impulse to start his tongue at her ankle and worked his way up each leg to her inner thigh.

She stopped him before he got too close to the meeting of her thighs. "Are you sure you're ready for what's there?" she asked him.

"It's OK," he assured her, "I'll only do what you want me to do." He continued his exploration up her other leg and moved to her ass. He pulled off her panties and discovered the most beautifully round ass he'd ever seen. He didn't know what he expected. His own ass was rounder than Ben's, but small. Hers was full and firm. He ran his tongue along the surface and then peaked into the dimple where her cheeks met at the top. Slowly, his tongue slid down until he was licking her asshole. This was something he swore he would never do, but he was enjoying the taste and feel of her body so much that he did not want to stop. He slid his tongue around the opening as she moaned, then he poked his tongue gently inside. He slid his tongue from the base of her ass to the top and down again in smooth motions. Raheed was so hard that he feared if he touched his dick, he would come immediately.

She slid underneath him so that they were face-to-face. He lifted her legs and reached for the lube on the coffee table. As he applied the lube to his dick and her ass, he kissed her while sliding himself inside her. Her tightness surrounded him in familiar ways. He pushed in, careful not to go too fast and waste the moment. He took the opportunity to run his tongue over her breasts. "Squeeze harder," she said. Raheed pulled at her nipple as she instructed, and she moved fast against him. He could not hold himself in anymore and came inside her.

Two weeks earlier, he confided in her about the money. "I have money. We can start a life together," Raheed blurted out as they were watching TV and eating ice cream after sex. He told her what he hadn't told anyone. Ben's dad offered him money to leave his son alone. He still had the check.

"What? Why wouldn't you lead with that?" She said, pulling him into the sweetest kiss he had ever felt.

But he couldn't bring himself to cash it. First, it made him feel sleazy. Second, it was't anything compared to money he could get from Ben over time. *Maybe it's time to take what I can get and leave,* he thought.

He went back to Ben's apartment for his check and his clothes. He would leave the way he came, with a duffle bag of clothes and nothing else. With the money he could buy his own car and computer, pay part of his tuition. *I can get loans for the rest,* he thought. The car was Ben's. *He can keep it,* Raheed thought.

When he walked in, Ben was sleeping on the couch in the clothes he had on the night before. It was clear he had waited up for him.

Raheed tried to quietly go to his room to pack.

"I'm glad to know you're OK. I wasn't up worried all night."

"Whatever," he said. "Where's your boyfriend?"

Raheed could tell Ben had been drinking from the way he slurred his words.

Ben got up and to make himself coffee. He could smell the perfume on Raheed all the way in the kitchen. He swallowed hard to keep himself from crying. He knew he didn't have a right to be hurt, but he was anyway.

"Brad and I decided to take a break."

"I don't believe that you broke up because I stormed out."

"No. It's because he made a deal with my father to go out with me."

"That sounds like your dad."

"I bet you know all about it."

"What in the hell are you talking about?"

"Did my dad pay you to leave?"

"Did you go through my things?" Raheed ran into his room and found the check still in the drawer. He breathed a sigh of relief.

"No. But I didn't have to," Ben lied, standing in the doorway to Raheed's room. "Why didn't you cash it already? Waiting for the right time?"

"Look, I was going to tell you. Your dad approached me when he found out I was living here and gave me a check. I wasn't going to cash it."

"Don't lie to me. You were going to take the money and run."

"Well, you know all about bribing people, don't you? Remember Kendra? She told me all about you."

"I figured she would, but you came back to me anyway and didn't say a word. What does that say about you?"

"I'm not like you or your family. Here, take your fucking money," Raheed balled up the check and threw it at him. "I'm going to forget I ever met you." He stuffed clothes into his bag.

Ben reached out to touch Raheed's shoulder. *He could be gone forever,* he thought. He didn't know if he could live with himself if he drove him away. "Don't go. I'm sorry," he said.

"Get off me," he said pushing Ben's arm off so hard he lost his balance.

"My father's an ass." Ben said holding on to the wall. "I'll never talk to him again if that will get you to stay."

"Here are your car keys."

"Keep the car."

"I don't want it or anything to do with you." Raheed left for the second time in two days. He walked to the bus stop, still fuming in righteous anger. He took some deep breaths, *Where am I going?* he wondered. *Back to Destiny? How can he go back there without any money? She was counting on that money to start a new life. Why did I give it back to him? Pride,* he thought. *I let my pride get in the way. So what if Ben thought that I was a con artist and a user? A hustler. Wasn't that what he was? He might as well be on a corner.* He called D'Shawn. "Can I stay with you a few days?"

"I fucked up," Raheed said, standing in D'Shawn's doorway.

"Come in and tell me all about it."

Raheed told him about the talk with Brad and his promise to Destiny and the check and how he ran away, again.

"I don't think this is so bad."

"Are you crazy? I left without the money. How dumb was that?"

"That was the smartest thing you've done so far. This proves that Ben means more to you than the money you can get out of him."

"I don't think he sees it like that."

"He'll blame his father, not you. If you took the money, he would have kicked you out instead of begged you to stay."

"I can't go back there, and I can't go to Destiny empty handed."

"Destiny is crazy enough to take you in any way."

"I don't want to be a burden on her."

"That's why you're going to stay here."

"I fucked up my life."

"Stop being so dramatic. Stay here for a few days. Let Ben get a little desperate and tell him that you still want to be friends. He'll keep things the way they were. Don't worry."

"I don't want to go back."

"Of course you don't. But you are a practical man and not going to throw away your future."

"And Destiny?"

"You will explain things to her. She'll understand."

"Destiny?"

"Hi. Did you get it?"

"I have something to tell you."

"Oh no. You took the money and you're on some beach somewhere without me." He could tell that she was only half-kidding.

"I gave it back to him."

She didn't say anything.

"Destiny? Are you still there?"

"I'm here. Why did you give it back?"

"He accused me of using him for his money."

"Aren't you?" It stung when she said it, even more than when Ben said it. "I don't mean to sound harsh, but it's time to come to terms with what's happening here. You're in this to get paid. I'm sorry to hurt your feelings, but you don't love a man that you have sex with for money. Own up to it. Do it, or not, but don't go around feeling guilty about it."

"I'm sorry," he said.

"I have to go."

"You sent Brad to me?" Ben barged in on his father's after-dinner cocktail time in his office at home.

"I figured that if you must have a man and you like the Black ones, I could at least give you one with a future."

"Give me? What is this, the nineteenth century?"

"Don't be so sensitive," his father bristled. "You know I didn't mean it like that."

"Stay out of my life, Dad. Don't call. Don't text, just leave me alone."

"You want to keep that apartment and the money though, right?"

"You owe me that much!" Ben said walking out of the office.

"Where have you been?" Ben asked. Raheed was sitting in the living room watching TV when he came back to the apartment.

"D'Shawn let me crash at his place."

Ben said a silent prayer of thanks. *At least he wasn't with that woman,* he thought. "You can come back here anytime," he said.

"Are you sure you won't kick me out the next time you get a boyfriend?"

"No one will ever run you away from here. I will move before I let that happen. The place is yours."

"I wish I could believe you."

"I'll put the lease in your name if it will make you feel better," Ben said knowing his father would never allow it. "Nothing has to change."

"I'm going to bed."

Ben nodded.

Ben came home to find a pretty brown-skinned girl with tight pants in the apartment. "Who's this?"

"Ben, this is Jade from my class. I left my bag and she's giving it back to me."

"Hi," she said, with a friendly smile.

Ben barely looked at her when he said, "Hey." She got the message and quickly gathered her stuff.

Ben ignored her movements and asked Raheed, "You want to go to dinner tonight?"

"We were about to go out," Raheed said, trying to keep Jade from leaving.

"Oh. I didn't know. Hey, I don't want to interrupt," Ben said, slamming the doors as he gathered ingredients from the kitchen cabinets.

Jade put her hands up. "Hey, I'll see you in class," she said rushing out of the apartment.

"What was that?" Raheed asked.

"What? I didn't say anything."

"You gave her some attitude."

Ben continued to make himself a quick meal. "I'm not trying to interfere with you going on a date. We had plans, that's all."

"What date?"

"She is clearly into you."

"Not now that you pissed all over me like I was your territory or something."

"I'm not having this conversation with you," Ben said, moving into the living room.

"Oh yeah. Well, I'm having it with you," Raheed said. "So what if she likes me. You fuck god knows how many other guys, but can't take it if someone looks my way. What do you want from me? Huh?," he said approaching Ben. Raheed grabbed his dick and pushed Ben into the kitchen, knocking his food out of his hands. "I'm talking to you. Is this what you want from me?" Raheed tried to pull in his anger, but the more he looked at Ben, the more he wanted to hurt him. "All I am is your own personal dick you can have any time you want. Huh?" He pushed him again, so hard he almost fell to the ground.

Raheed was scaring him. Ben was afraid that he would punch him at any second. He didn't want to fight with him. Ben knew he would lose.

"You want me to fuck you," Raheed said. "That's all you ever want from me."

"Raheed that's not true. You know I love you."

"Shut up," he said pushing Ben back against the kitchen counter. Before he could recover from the push, Raheed turned him around and bent him over the counter. Raheed quickly unbuckled his pants and let them fall to the floor. Ben heard Raheed's belt and saw his hand groping around the counter and grabbing a bottle of olive oil. Ben felt Raheed slide oil on his asshole. He entered hard and angry.

"Is this what you want from me?"

Ben knew it was an important question, full of meaning despite the circumstances. He couldn't think straight. The feel of Raheed's hands on his waist and back, his dick thumping against his prostate blocked all rational thought. It had been so long. "Yes," was all he managed to say. Raheed came fast, but he lasted long enough for Ben to come on his own a few seconds later.

Raheed zipped up and went directly into his room, leaving Ben dripping of cum and oil and some thin squirts of shit. The combination slicked his ass and the back of his thighs. He had not been ready for Raheed. He took off all his clothes in the middle of the kitchen and made his way to the shower. The warm water soothed his sore muscles. He felt electricity up and down his spine as he recalled the events of a few minutes earlier. His asshole still burned from what Raheed did to him. He had been rough with him, taken him without permission. It reminded him of being underneath him in his bed in the frat house. Raheed would push him on the bed, yank his pants down and enter him fast and hard. It was as if he was on a mission to come and Ben was there to reap the benefits. After it was over Raheed would collect his money and leave without a lot of talking. Ben did not complain about the sex, but he wanted Raheed to stay. He didn't have to hold him, just stay and talk. When he did stay, it was a gift like the day he finally kissed him. There was nothing better than that first kiss.

Raheed lay on his bed in a ball. He was not proud of what he did. He could see the fear in Ben's eyes. He was so angry. Angry at Ben for wanting too much from him. Angry at himself for staying when he knew it was not right. He did not love Ben. He loved Destiny, but he had nothing to offer her.

Ben slid into bed, naked. He put his back to Raheed and let him hold him. "This is all I ever wanted," Ben said.

"I know."

D'Shawn came into the café with mirrored shades. They greeted each other. Raheed noticed that he did not take them off when he sat down. "So, how have you been? You haven't been picking up your phone lately."

"I've been busy," D'Shawn said. "One foot in front of the other, keeping in step."

"Where did you go this month? Milan?"

"Marseille."

"I hope you had a good time." Ben felt that D'Shawn was not himself. Usually, he had to struggle to get a word in. "What's up, man? You OK?"

"Everything's good."

Raheed looked closer at D'Shawn's face and realized that the color of his cheek wasn't right. Too grey. "What's up with your face?"

"Look, I didn't come here for the third degree. What's going on with you? Did you get this guy to marry you yet? You are this close to a serious payoff."

Raheed continued to study D'Shawn's cheek. "That's a bruise! What the fuck is going on?"

"Keep your voice down. It's nothing I can't handle."

"Are you crazy? Is he paying you enough to let him kick your ass?"

"As a matter of fact, he is."

Raheed shook his head.

"Don't look at me like that. One or two more payments from this guy and I'm out. I have enough invested that I can retire. Go to college like you. Get my own home, that's really mine. Raheed, don't judge me like that. I don't judge you. That's what our friendship is based on. If I didn't have that, I don't know what I'd do."

"I would never judge you," he said, reaching across the table to hold D'Shawn's hand. "I just want you to be OK." Raheed leaned in and whispered, "If we need to put this white man 6 feet under, I'm with you."

"Now that's friendship!" D'Shawn laughed, but then put his hand on his face to soothe the pain.

They barely spoke. They went to classes, Raheed went to his work-study job and studied at the kitchen table. Ben studied in the living room. Their class schedules were opposite, so they didn't run into each other very often. Ben was out of the house before Raheed had to get ready to leave. One night, Ben had an exam he finished early and Raheed's class was canceled. The two were in the house at the same time. Destiny was visiting her mother.

"Do you want to order out?" Raheed asked.

"I'll just have leftovers."

"Yeah, I'll have that, too." They ate in silence. Raheed was not used to quiet. His family always talked at dinner when he was little, then his aunt's house was full of kids and there were lots of other kids at the center. "You know what I would like for dessert?"

"Ice cream?" Ben said relieved to be talking again.

"How did you know?"

"You made me stop for ice cream sometimes when we used to meet in my car, remember?"

"Oh, yeah. I bet you don't remember my favorite flavor."

"Rocky Road. What's mine?"

"Strawberry. I remember because what grown man likes strawberry? That's like, for little girls."

"Hey. The manliest of men like strawberry. Professional football players like strawberry."

"Name one."

"Khalil Mack."

Raheed laughed for the first time in weeks. "You are so crazy. You have no idea what flavor Khalil Mack likes."

"If you don't believe me, read some of his interviews," Ben pretended to search on his phone. "I can't find it now, but it's there."

"I would like to go back to that shop sometime. They have the best ice cream. But I can't go right now. I have to study for a test tomorrow."

"I'll get it. The drive will clear my head."

"Are you sure?" Raheed asked.

"Of course," Ben reflexively kissed him on the forehead.

"Hello."

"Do you know a Ben Parker?" The voice on the other end of the phone was a woman. She sounded very official.

"Yeah, who are you?"

"You were his emergency contact."

"What happened?" Raheed's heart began to pound.

"There has been an accident, sir."

"What? Is he dead?" Dead. That word. He hated that word. His aunt found those cops on her doorstep when his parents died. The highway patrol. He could hear them from the kitchen table.

"No sir, but he's pretty banged up."

Raheed let out a sigh of relief and realized he had been holding his breath since the call began.

"He's at Windsor Memorial if you want to see him."

"What happened? What does that mean banged up?"

"His car was hit by a drunk driver. That's all I know. You will have to ask the doctors more about that."

"What? Wait. Don't hang–" There was silence. It suddenly hit him. What if Ben dies? He called D'Shawn.

"Ben's been a car accident."

"Oh man, I'm sorry. Is he OK?

"D'Shawn, what if he dies?"

"You can't think like that."

Raheed was almost dizzy with emotions. His voice cracked, "I don't want him to die."

"Don't worry about that now. Get off the phone with me and go to the hospital. Did you call his folks?"

"I don't have their number."

"Well, they must have found you through his phone. He will have it. Go to the hospital, call his parents and importantly, stay with him. You can't afford to not be there when he wakes up."

"His father hates me. His family is not going to let me be with him."

"Look, you're his partner, right? You have a right to be there."

"I'm not, though. We're just talking again right now."

"The hospital doesn't know that. Look man. This is serious. You have it good with him. Fight for what's yours."

"Mine? I will be working for him."

"He's rich. Do you love him?"

"I care about him. I don't want anything bad to happen to him."

"Can you keep sleeping with him?"

"I don't mind it. It's good. Really good sometimes."

"There you go. What more do you need?"

"Shouldn't I feel more than that?"

"Look, man, there are worse arrangements."

"What about Destiny?"

"I don't know, but you won't have Ben if you don't go right now."

On the way to the hospital, Raheed was plagued with worry about Ben, about himself and what kind of future he couldn't have with Destiny if he pursued Ben. *This is all my fault,* he thought. *He was going to get me ice cream.* Then, he had another devastating thought: *If he dies, then I won't be anywhere. It's all his. The apartment, the car. Even his tuition. It's like he owns me.* But he also realized in another way, he would be free.

When he got to the hospital, Ben was unconscious. His head was wrapped in bandages, both of his eyes were black and blue, his right arm was in a cast, and he had on a mask to help him breathe. He was glad that Ben was unconscious because then he couldn't feel Raheed's palms sweating. If he was going to do this, he had to be all in. After about an hour of checking with the nurses, the doctor came to give an update on Ben's condition.

When the doctor finally showed up, he looked at Raheed beside Ben's bed as if he were unsure if he should give him the information and said, "Who are you?"

Raheed paused for a second and gathered himself to looked into the doctor's eyes and said, "I'm his partner." Saying it didn't feel as bad as he expected it to. D'Shawn was right, he had to fight for what was his. He earned his place next to Ben and it didn't matter what anybody else thought, not his family or Ben's. He sat down next to the bed and held Ben's hand.

"He is going to be alright, but we have to get him into surgery. He has some internal bleeding, but I think he will recover quickly. I have to get his next of kin to sign off on these release papers. Is that you?"

Right then the father walked in. "The hell he is!" Ben's father stomped into the room with his sister and stepmother trailing behind him.

"What are you doing here?" Ben's father growled at Raheed.

"Dad!" Ben's sister said.

"Don't 'dad' me," he said. "This is for family only. For all I know he was hit trying to do some favor for you," he said gesturing to Raheed.

"Look, I don't want to do this with you right now," Raheed said. "The most important thing is Ben. I'm his partner and I have a right to be here."

"I thought you two broke up when you went to jail," Ben's father scoffed.

"Things change." Raheed smiled, knowing it would drive Ben's father mad.

Before the elder Parker could say anything else, the doctor cleared his throat. Running his fingers through his hair the doctor said, "I'll leave it to you to decide if this man should be here or not," pointing to Raheed. "Ben needs surgery and time is running out. So, who is going to sign these papers?"

Raheed recognized Ben's sister Melanie. She gave him a hug and spoke up. "This is Ben's partner. He should be here."

Ben's father added, "Well until he puts a ring on your finger, I'm still his next of kin. I can't believe I'm saying that about a man," he said to his wife, who nodded in agreement. "Give me that paperwork."

Ben's father snatched the clipboard from the doctor's hands. "Let's get this going!"

"I already knew about her," Ben was standing in his father's home office. His arm was still in a cast, but he was able to stand and walk without crutches. His father informed him that Destiny was still in Raheed's life.

"No, you didn't. I can tell by the look on your face."

"You don't think you're the only one who has him followed, do you? After all, I am your son."

"Idiot!"

"You and mom were so unhappy. You were seeing every woman in your own social circle, and she sat around being humiliated but saying nothing. You think she didn't know? I don't want it to be like that between Raheed and me. Everything is out in the open. He blows off a little steam once and a while, and I have peace of mind that I know what's going on. And I can have my own dalliances if I want to, but we always come home to each other. That's the agreement."

"You're a fucking doormat," his father scoffed. "Haven't you learned anything about being a Parker? You're getting used, son. If he was banging every guy in town, I could see what you're saying. I would still think it's stupid, but I could see it. It's been only her for six months now. He loves this man, woman—can't you see that? I guess it's a she these days. Whatever. It can give him things you can't. Whatever kind of lifestyle you choose, I still love you and you are still my son. I don't want to see you get hurt."

"You mean you don't want me to embarrass you."

"Believe what you want, just think about this before you get yourself into something you can't get out of."

"I have. We got married over the weekend. This is something you can't escape. It's already happened. We're going to be a happy family."

ANGEL

OF

MERCY

2016

John was enjoying his club soda and lime. He sat in a booth with his back against the wall. John liked to people watch. At the Thaxton, he was never disappointed. There was nothing like an old brown bar. Exposed brick, walnut hand-crafted bar, leather barstools. Everything had aged by years of use by thousands of bar patrons. Through economic downturns, exuberant birthday celebrations that turned ugly, excited bachelor and bachelorette parties that went too far. The bar had history. If it had been just 30 years ago, he probably would have had a hard time getting in at all unless he knew a white person in the bar. With each sip of his drink, he soaked in the entire history of the space. It was once the preferred spot for factory workers at the Brown Shoe company and tobacco companies who regularly held bare-knuckle fights in the back alley to establish once and for all who were the kings of the city. It was a speakeasy during Prohibition, a gentleman's club, where ladies of the evening helped young executives unwind, a jazz bar, a micro-brewery that was a little too specialized, even for hipster tastes, and now an authentic piece of old St. Louis for the youngish professionals who wanted to touch something old in a world where everything has been renovated new. He felt all of this as an electric current slowly moving from his fingers to toes, up through his arms and legs, coursing throughout his body like a calm, internal river.

They played light 90s R&B over the sound system—no hip hop, nothing that could qualify as oldies, but old enough to touch on the teenage nostalgia for the majority of patrons. John saw the white man he'd come there for across the bar. The man was tall and muscular with light brown/blonde hair. The man was with his friends and girlfriend. They were loud and boisterous. It's clear that they are grown-up frat boy kind of men and former sorority girl girlfriends. John waited for the perfect time to touch his target. All he needed was a light brush against the arm, a hand on the shoulder. John ordered a beer and walked by the man and his friends. As he walked, he brushed up against his elbow a little, almost spilling his drink.

"I didn't get you, did I?" John asked.

"No, man."

"OK. Good." John took a seat at the bar.

In just the fraction of a second the two made contact, John implanted the idea that he was an interesting person. As a result, the man visually searched for John and found him in the bar.

The man, leaned over to his girlfriend, "I'm going to get another beer. Can I get you anything?"

"Nope," she said, giving him a peck on the cheek.

"OK. Be right back." He walked over the bar where man that bumped into him was sitting.

"Hey. I'm sorry again for bumping into you back there. My name is John."

"Brian." They shook hands, increasing Brian's interest in John. It happened without him noticing. Brian gestured to the bartender, "Can I get a beer over here?"

"Nice to meet you, Brian. Looks like you're having fun over there."

"Yeah. I just got a promotion at work." Brian spoke to him like he was disinterested in the conversation, even irritated. But John knows it was because he didn't know what to do with the sudden attention he wanted to pay to another man. He could feel the conflict in Brian's mind. The push and pull. Part of him wanted to walk away with his drink, but a growing part of him wanted to stay.

"Oh, yeah? What do you do?" John asked.

"I'm an editor. I just got promoted to managing editor. I started out as the copyeditor out of college." To Brian, John smelled faintly of lemon oil and lavender. He breathed in deeply. He liked the smell. It drew him in. His eyes lingered on John's body. He noticed that John had the smoothest skin he'd ever seen. It was medium brown and even though he seemed older than him, probably in his 40s even, he didn't have a line on his face. He was short and thin, but his body was tight and muscular. At least what he could make out under his shirt.

"Oh really? Look. I'm a graphic designer, but I'm working on a graphic novel. I'm looking for a good copyeditor."

"I don't really do that kind of work freelance."

"Well, take my card. If you ever want a freelance gig. give me a call."

Brian took the card and absentmindedly put it in his pocket. He found himself wanting to talk more. He felt as if he could listen to him talk forever.

"Are you an artist?"

"Well, I guess I am now with this book happening. I used to want to be an artist, but…"

"But what?"

"It's a hard to do full time. Now I get to be creative on other people's projects."

"But it's not the same, huh?"

"Yeah. The book is a good way to get back to what I love."

Brian smiled and the more he talked to John the happier he felt. Like a warm glow all over his body. The feeling made him not want to look at John. His heart raced and his palms became sweaty. John's voice did something to his brain. He could feel himself reaching out to John with his thoughts. Soaking up his smell. He had to get away. "Where's that beer?" he yelled at the bartender, who pointed out that his beer was already on the counter with a look that said, "Fuck you, jerk."

John touched Brian's arm and a shock of arousal struck him. "Shouldn't you get back to your party?" John pointed to Brian's finance and friends who were waving at him to come back. Brian was so startled that he almost fell off the barstool.

"See you later man," he said to John, forcing himself to look away. He thought it would be easier to walk away if he didn't look at him, but John's face filled his thoughts despite himself. On his way back to the table he went over John in his mind. He has smooth brown skin. No beard. He wondered what it would be like to lightly stroke his hand on John's chin.

"That beer took a long time," said his finance, Jordan.

"Yeah. I don't know what was going on with that bartender." He looked back to see if John was still there as Jordan hugged his right arm, but he was gone.

John sat at his desk in his loft. The exposed beams and the brick wall made him feel like he was in Brooklyn as opposed to St. Louis. He pulled out his cast iron pot and sprinkled a dusting of white powder inside. He added some loose leaves of white tea, a few cups of water, and put it on the stove. Once the simple concoction had boiled, he poured it into a clear glass cup. The leaves swirled and floated to the top. He blew on the liquid and thought of Brian. In the teacup, he could see Brian pacing in his apartment on the other side of town. John closed his eyes. He concentrated on Brian's thoughts. Blowing into the cup, he also blew the image of his face and voice into Brian's mind.

I'm going crazy. This is silly. Brian stood in front of the window and looked down onto the street. People passed with their kids and dogs. He liked the edge of town; it was quiet and he was able to get his work done. He began to relax. He must be tired. "I'm fine," he said. His mind wandered and he saw the softness of John's brown eyes. He felt a warmth rise inside him when he thought of John's hands reaching out to touch his arm.

"What's going on?" Jordan walked in. "Are you OK? You look a little lost."

"What, me? Never. Just looking at the neighborhood."

She wrapped her arms around his waist, and he moved away. "Well, it's time for bed and I have something to give you for your promotion," she said smiling.

Brian got the hint, and they went into the bedroom. He kissed Jordan and touched her, but his mind was still fighting John's face and hands. He had only spoken to him for a few minutes, but the sound of John's voice stayed with him as he fell asleep and into the next day. Brian could not sit still. He fingered the business card over and over, unconsciously rubbing it. The thought of calling John was overpowering his other ideas, slowly nudging out everything else in his brain. Unable to stop, he found himself dialing the number on the card.

"Hello?" John's voice simultaneously made him feel relieved and anxious. He did not know what he was going to say, only that he had to call. "Hello? Is there someone there?"

"Yes," Brian croaked. "I'm sorry. It's me, Brian, from the other night."

"I'm sorry, I don't remember…"

The idea that John did not remember him hurt his feelings, but he couldn't understand why it had such an impact on him. "I was at the bar last night with friends and you bumped into me…"

John said nothing on the other side of the phone, increasing Brian's anxiety. He suddenly thought, *what if he doesn't want to talk to me?* He quickly searched his mind for something that would jog John's memory. "You said that you were looking for a copyeditor?" Brian closed his eyes and hoped that it would spark conversation.

"The copyeditor from the other night! Yes. I am looking for one for my graphic novel."

Brian opened his eyes and mouthed, "Yes!" and did a small dance in his chair. "Good," he said trying to sound nonchalant. "I'm looking for some freelance work and thought of you." None of this was true. He was swamped at work and did not want any extra, but if it would get him closer to John, he would find the time.

"OK. Well, how about we meet? Thursday evening? We can have coffee or something."

"Sure," Brian said quickly. "Let's meet at the Coffee Time at 7?"

John agreed and hung up. Brian tapped out drumroll on his desk in victory. He did it. They were going to meet. He went over the details of their conversation in his mind. A million questions raced through his thoughts. *Did I sound desperate? I stammered around for a while at the beginning, could he tell I was reaching for a way to talk to him? Did I sound sincere?*

"What's up dude?" He had been unaware that other people were watching him while he was on the phone, he didn't think of anyone else, just John.

"Looks like you got good news." His co-worker and friend, Stan, was waiting to know what was going on.

"Oh that," he smiled and put John's card back in his pocket. "I just secured a part-time thing working on a guy's graphic novel as a copyeditor." He swiftly decided that the truth was better than trying to keep up with lies.

"I didn't know you were looking for extra work," Stan looked concerned.

"Oh, it's nothing. I'm trying to save up for a ring for Jordan and this opportunity came up," he lied.

"Sweet. Good planning. I wish I had a girl like Jordan to save for. You're a lucky man, bro."

"Yeah, I am." Brian smiled as Stan went back to his desk.

Talking to Stan brought him back to his senses. He went back to working on the new issue of the magazine where he worked. It was a special issue on schools. "Who's Protecting the Children?" was in bold letters and a picture of a group of multiracial kids on the front. Brian took the picture himself at the playground near his house. He was proud of the picture. The articles were on promoting school voucher programs, protecting children from transsexuals in bathrooms and giving the youth hope for a brighter future in American oil and chemical companies. He believed in every word, but he couldn't concentrate on it. It took him until the early hours of the morning to finish what usually took him a few hours. Jordan called the office line a few times to check in on him. He also realized that she was making sure he was really in the office, though he never cheated on her before. When he finally got home, he fell asleep on the couch, with his clothes and shoes on.

John added a couple of ice cubes to a tall glass and poured some hot tea in the glass. The ice cracked and popped with the contact of the hot water. Brian dreamt that John stood over him, smiling. Brian sleepily looked up from the couch to see John's smiling face. His heart pounded in his chest. He was so excited that he popped up to greet him. John immediately pushed him back down onto the couch. Brian laughed playfully. John put his finger to his lips and shook his head, indicating for Brian to be quiet. Brian suppressed a giggle with his hand. He was vaguely aware that Jordan was asleep in the other room, but he didn't care. John gestured for him to lay on his back, and Brian complied. John gently guided his head so that his head was hanging down off the edge of the seat, while the rest of his body remained on the couch. Luckily, Brian had a couch that didn't have an armrest at each end, so he was comfortable. John unbuttoned Brian's shirt and slid his fingers on his bare chest, making Brian's dick jump to attention. Brian closed his eyes while one hand caressed his chest, the other expertly slipped his pointer and middle fingers down his throat. He went to rub his dick and John swatted his hand away. Brian moaned with pleasure. Before he knew what was happening John slid his dick into Brian's mouth. John firmly told him to open wide and he stretched his mouth so far it burned. Brian was not entirely surprised that he had John's dick in his mouth, he was shocked at how far down the back of his throat he could take it without his gag reflex taking over. John grunted as he pushed deeper and deeper into him. Sooner than Brian wanted him to, John began to buck and push like he was going cum. Brian could no longer breathe. He didn't want John to pull out. His dick was so sweet, and Brian was doing such a good job at deep throating him. Soon, he couldn't wait anymore to breathe and started to pull away, but John grabbed his head and forced his dick further down Brian's throat. Brian's body revolted into spasms from lack of oxygen, even though Brian never wanted it to end.

Finally, he felt a flash of hot liquid down his throat, and he struggled to swallow. Just when he thought he couldn't take it anymore, he felt Jordan's hands on his shoulders, shaking him awake. He took a deep breath like he was coming up from air after a long swim in the ocean.

"Brian! Are you OK? Are you having a nightmare?" Jordan looked almost ready to call 911.

He found himself hanging half off the couch, legs over the back and his torso almost to the floor. Jordan was struggling to help him get back onto the couch.

Jordan had lots of questions that he didn't have the answer to. Why didn't he come to bed when he got home? Why was he in such a strange position? Had he been drinking? Or high? He tried to explain the evening, but it came up short, for him too. Brian was not sure about anything. She brought him some water. His hands were shaking. His throat was sore. He felt water drip down his chest and realized that his shirt was fully unbuttoned and open.

"Excuse me," he said, simultaneously giving Jordan the glass of water, pushing her aside as he went into the bathroom. Brian checked himself out in the mirror. He didn't have any marks on him. He seemed fine other than wild hair and red eyes. He looked like he had been through an adventure. He felt oddly excited and wanted more. When he went to pee, he saw that he had cum in his pants. Then the memory of his dream flooded his senses. The sweet smell and taste of John's dick and cum, the feel of his balls against his forehead, the overwhelming desire to please him, so much so that it made his skin feel hot. He choked on the pleasure of making John happy. It filled him and the bathroom. He was hard again. The more Brian thought about John's fingers running up and down his chest and holding his head, demanding submission, the more his dick demanded to be stroked. He came holding his breath in front of the mirror.

When he emerged from the bathroom, Jordan was dressed for work and drinking coffee. All concern was wiped from her face, and she looked suspicious. "Are you having an affair?"

"What? No!"

"Well, I heard you in there choking it out. Are you going to tell me you were thinking of me?"

Brian didn't know what to say. He didn't know why he was doing these things. What was he going to say to his fiancé? "I met a homo-sexual yesterday and now I dream of having him face fuck me on the couch?"

"Look, I'm sorry. I came home late, crashed on the couch and now I was just letting off a little steam." He saw that his explanation was not working for he and added, "I got home, drank some ungodly concoction that Stan told me about and fell asleep. It messed me up bad." Jordan sighed in relief.

"You know you can't drink the hard stuff! What were you think-ing? I've got an early meeting. Don't forget we're having dinner with my parents tonight." She grabbed her keys and bags and glided out of the door. Brian didn't have time to eat. He quickly rinsed off, shaved, and scrambled out the door.

Brian took deep breaths. *It's OK. I'm just going to meet with him to-morrow and find out about this job. That's not weird. It's all perfectly normal.* Soon, he began to convince himself that everything was all OK. Nothing was out of the ordinary. Brian put John to the back of his mind and concentrated on the work that had been piling up for the past few days. He tried to catch up the day before but was distracted and disorganized. Eventually, he was able to get some work done in the afternoon.

For the rest of the day, Brian fought thoughts about John. He went to the special single-stall bathroom in the basement and jacked off and imagined that John walked into the bathroom and pushed his shoulders down, forcing him onto his knees. He eagerly opened his mouth wide. John shook the head of his dick and told him to kiss it. He gently held the beautiful brown dick, shades darker than the rest of his skin, kissing it up and down the shaft, licking the salt off his balls before pulling John's dick into his mouth by grabbing onto his ass. Brian looked up to see John's eyes closed and head back in ecstasy. He worked John's dick with his tongue, fervently slurping and sucking until John grabbed his head and pushed hard and deep down his throat. Brian couldn't breathe. John's grip on the back of his head was firm while he thrust his dick further down his throat. Brian's eyes began to tear as he resisted the urge to pull away. When he thought he couldn't hold on any longer, John pushed himself so deep down Brian's throat that his tongue touched John's balls.

"Lick!" John ordered and Brian complied. Licking and slurping as much as he could. His eyes streamed tears and his lungs burned. He fought the urge to vomit as he tried to swallow as John came in his throat. He had to let it flow out of his mouth in order let John finish with a clean dick. Brian felt accomplished and satisfied just listening to John scream with pleasure. When John finally released him right before he felt he would pass out. He gasped for air, licking up excess cum in between gulps of air.

"Good boy," John said.

Brian emerged from the bathroom ready to work again for a while until thoughts of John creeped in again. Brian was under pressure to finish editing by the deadline. He tried to concentrate on the words, but they kept moving around on the page. Words like "parental choice," "personal responsibility," and "only two genders" floated around on the page. He skipped around between the articles he was responsible for editing, moving in between lines, and sliding around the punctuation. The words were a jumble in his head. By the time he got to the piece entitled, "The Forgotten Crime of Black-On-Black Violence," his head was pounding. He had written that one himself. He wanted to highlight crime statistics that showed Black people killed each other far more often than the police killed them. In fact, the police were doing them a favor and probably preventing future crimes when they took down criminals. He just needed to check it over and pass it on to another editor to make sure it was ready, but his head felt like it was being cracked open with a hammer. He found that his head eased when he thought about John. The thought of his face soothed Brian's aching temples.

Brian wound up having to stay late to get even a little bit done. His phone rang; it was Jordan.

"Hey, where are you?"

"I'm just finishing up here. I'll be home in a few—"

"Are you serious? Did you forget the dinner with my parents?"

"Shit! I forgot. I'm sorry. I'll be right there." He paused, "Where are we meeting again?"

The restaurant was only a few blocks away from Brian's office. On the way, he hummed a little tune that he didn't recognize and assumed he made up on the spot. Brian's mood was light, and he smiled to himself thinking of the coffee date he would have the next night with John. He went over his clothes selection in his head. He frowned thinking that none of it seemed appropriate. His day at work was going to be busy the next day. With the addition of dinner with his future in-laws, he was not going to have time to run and get something new to wear the next evening. He wouldn't even have a chance to dry clean his favorite shirt. He thought that there was probably an all-night dry cleaner in the city. *Maybe he could go after dinner, or better, after Jordan went to sleep so she wouldn't ask questions.* He stopped to look up dry cleaners on his phone when he felt a hand on his shoulder. He jumped.

"Looking for the restaurant?" It was Jordan. "You're standing right in front of it. What's the matter with you, today?"

"Working too hard I guess," he said, erasing the search screen on his phone so that Jordan would not see that he was looking for cleaners.

Throughout dinner Brian felt back to his old self. He liked Jordan's parents. Her father was a retired construction manager. He specialized in big projects like dams and highway construction. Her mother was a retired schoolteacher. They lived in Nebraska but visited their 5 children often because they had the time. They were easy to spend time with. Her mother was a bit opinionated, but he usually agreed with her, so they got along fine.

The four of them spent the evening eating engaging in small talk. The only thing that threatened Brian's feeling normal was the waiter. He was dark skinned—darker than John—shorter than average and round in the middle. Brian noticed that he was beginning to bald around the temples, but he didn't look to be more than 35. The waiter spent the night making small mistakes, forgetting the appetizer order, bringing the wrong salad dressing, spilling a glass of water. Brian caught him taking long looks out the windows like he was counting down the seconds until his shift would be over.

"I can't believe him," Jordan's mother said. Jordan and her father nodded in agreement, but Brian realized he had missed part of the conversation.

"I should make a complaint to the manager," Jordan's mother said.

"Mom, let it go."

"When I pay these kinds of prices, I expect better service than this." her father agreed with his wife.

Brian suddenly felt as if he had spent the evening at another table. "What happened?" he asked and immediately regretted it.

"Where have you been all night? That black family has gotten their food before us, even though they came in 10 minutes later. They also seem to be getting lively conversation from our waiter, not the sour expression we've been getting."

"So, what are you thinking is wrong?" Brian asked, getting a little hot. He wondered if someone had turned up the heat.

"Reverse racism, of course," Jordan's father chimed in. "He clearly doesn't value us as much as customers."

Brian's headache returned. It started out like a little pain when they sat down, but it was growing into a full-on migraine on his left temple.

"With a name like La'Quan it's a wonder he was able to take down our orders at all." Jordan and her father laughed at her mother's joke.

"Mom, you know you are not supposed to say things like that. He can't help his name."

"Well, I can't help if it's ridiculous. Let's reflect his attitude in his tip."

"No!" Brian said a little more forcefully than he meant to. His head was throbbing, and he was beginning to feel dizzy. He just wanted to leave. He quickly smiled as casually as he could. He didn't want everyone to know how ill he felt.

"I mean, there's probably a good explanation for it," Brian said. "Let's give him the benefit of the doubt." Everyone at the table stared at him. "What?" he asked. "Why are you all looking at me like that?" His face was burning hot, and the heat was spreading down his body.

"Usually, you would be the first one to agree with mom," Jordan said.

"It's not that I don't agree with you Patricia," he said. "But you know, I used to wait tables in college, and I lived on tips, so I may have a soft spot here. Excuse me." He got up from the table and wondered if Jordan would catch him in his lie. She knew every job he ever had. He was confident he could lie some more if he had to. *I'll worry about that later. Right now,* he thought, *I have to get to the bathroom and splash some cold water over my face.*

He walked quickly back to the bathroom. On the way, he heard a crash in the kitchen and saw their waiter bending down to clean up his spill and saw that he had a little cleavage under his shirt. The softness of the waiter's chest aroused Brian sightly. He could also hear L'Quan being yelled at by the manager. Brian went into a stall to gather his thoughts. The bathroom smelled of a lemon-scented cleanser that made him want to vomit. He heard someone else come into the bathroom. Soft, muffled sounds echoed through bathroom. He opened the door to see their waiter wiping away tears.

La'Quan looked up at Brian's reflection in the mirror. "It's been one of those days," he said with a meager smile.

Brian reached out and touched his shoulder. He silently moved closer, and the waiter turned toward him. Brian pulled the waiter close to him and La'Quan rested his head on Brian's shoulder. Brian wrapped his arms around him. The two swayed a little to their own internal music. Brian felt like he was in a fog watching himself holding the waiter. It felt intimate, but not awkward. The two stood in each other's arms, gently moving together until they heard the door of the restroom open. Both men recoiled from each other like they had suddenly burst into flames. The other customer stopped at the door, not knowing if he should enter. The waiter excused himself and quickly exited. Not knowing what else to do, Brian washed his hands and left the bathroom.

Brian was sweating through his shirt. He was sure his face was red and his hands trembled. *You can do this. It's OK. You're not going crazy. You're just overworked. Maybe a cold.* He took careful steps back to the table.

"I got this," he said to no one in particular.

The way that Jordan and her parents looked at him let him know that he was not hiding his condition well.

Jordan looked at him like he was dying before her eyes. "What happened?" she said, standing up.

"Nothing. I just went to the bathroom. Everything's fine." He sat back down at the table. His head was spinning.

"Don't tell me everything's fine son," her father said. You look like you've seen a ghost. "What went on between here and the bathroom?"

"I'm...I'm just not feeling well. I think I have a stomach flu. Maybe we should pay the check and go."

"Sure, honey," Jordan said, rubbing his back and trying to steady him as he stood up.

Nothing seemed real to Brian. The walls started to buckle and all the voices around him gradually quieted to a whisper, and then he was in the back of an ambulance.

Jordan was sitting at his feet, rubbing his leg. She was saying, "It's going to be OK." There was an EMT putting in an IV into his arm. Everything was swirling until he threw up all over the EMT. The next thing he remembered was being in a hospital room with Jordan standing over him. "Hey," she said, the moment he opened his eyes. "Don't try to move. The doctor will be back with your blood test in a minute."

"What happened?" he asked. Even in his reduced state he knew was a stupid question.

"They're not sure. We are going to find out, OK? Don't worry."

"I feel fine now. Just a little sleepy, but I'm OK."

"Well, then go to sleep. I'll wake you if anything interesting happens."

He drifted off and the next time he opened his eyes the waiter from the restaurant was standing at the foot of his bed.

"Hi," the waiter said. He had a worried smile. "I hoped you would wake soon."

"Where's Jordan?"

"Who? Don't worry, baby. We'll get this all taken care of."

Brian tried to sit up, but he was too dizzy. "Get what taken care of? Where's my fiancé?" The smell of lemons filled the air.

The waiter looked down and then at the doctor, who Brian just noticed was standing beside the waiter. "This is what I'm telling you, Doc. It's like he doesn't remember who he is."

"What? I know who I am. I'm Brian Eppler. I am 30 years old. I live in St. Louis and I work as an editor at the Conservative Republic magazine."

The waiter smiled meekly. "Good. All those things used to be true, honey. Now, who am I?"

"The waiter from last night. The one from the bathroom. We... uh...I don't know."

"That's how we met two years ago. What's my name?"

"Your name?" He struggled to remember the waiter's name tag, but then he realized it was still on his shirt. It was fuzzy at first and he had to sit up to get a clear picture. "John?"

"Yes!" John was standing where the waiter had been. "He is going to be alright, doctor. This is much better than yesterday."

John walked over to the side and kissed him on the lips. Brian closed his eyes and kissed him back. John's arms circled around his neck. "I'm so glad you're better, baby. I can take you home and you can get back to work. The guys at RQ are worried about you. They missed you at the Black Lives Matter rally."

"RQ?"

"Radical Queers. Um…Baby do you still have a fever?" John touched the back of his hand to Brian's forehead. "I'm going to get the nurse to—."

"No, don't go," Brian pulled John back to the bed. "Stay. Tell me more about the group."

He didn't understand what John was talking about, but he didn't want him to go. He was comforted by his presence. John put his hand on Brian's chest and told him more about these people he never met, but Brian didn't care, he was just happy that John was there.

"Well, Sharlene is threatening to bake a cake, and you know how well her cupcakes went over last time. I think I'll try to convince her to buy one instead. And of course, La'Quan sends his love." John smelled good, like lemon soap and coconut oil. John kissed his cheeks and his neck. Brian felt so at home with him. He let himself sink into the bed under John's tender touch and voice. Everything felt like it should be.

Brian's eyelids were getting heavier. He could hear John's voice say, "Rest, baby. I'll be right back."

Brian tried to say, "Don't go," but his mouth felt like it was full of glue. He went to reach out for him, but he could not move his limbs. All he could do was let sleep take him again. When Brian woke up, he felt a hand on his arm. He tried to touch the hand and found that he could move again. "I'm glad you stayed," he said.

"I'm not going anywhere." Jordan's voice filled the room. Brian sat up and looked around for John.

"Hey, don't try to get up," she said, gently guiding him to lay down again.

"You've been out for about 12 hours." Jordan was smiling. She had dark rings around her eyes and her hair needed shampoo. She had obviously spent the night in the hospital room.

It was the same hospital room as in his dream, only there were more details. He looked around and saw his jacket from the night at the restaurant draped over the back of a chair. Jordan's bag sat on the table next to the bed. His shoes were under the window in the corner. He felt a crushing disappointment. *I think this one is real. I'm back,* he thought.

"We were so worried about you," Jordan said.

"What happened?"

"You came back from the restroom, looking like hell and then you fainted. My mother thinks it's from the food at the restaurant. There was nothing but Africans working in the kitchen, and I read an article online that said they don't follow the same sanitary standards as we do."

"What did the doctor say? Was it food poisoning?" He was beginning to get a headache again.

"They said it wasn't clear, but what else could it be? The good news is that we were just waiting until you woke up to do a few more tests. If they find nothing, they'll discharge you." She smiled, "My mother is sure we have a good case against the restaurant. We will sue the bastards, don't worry."

"Please, don't. I think I was just exhausted from working so hard."

"They can't get away with—" Jordan stopped as Brian squeezed his eyes shut and held his head. She saw that the conversation was upsetting him and changed the subject.

His pain subsided after a while. Brian noticed a half-eaten slice of lemon cake on the nightstand.

"I'm starving."

"That's good. The doctor says an appetite is a good sign."

"What day is it?"

"Thursday," she answered.

Brian thought, *John. I'm supposed to meet him tonight. I've got to get out of here. He's going to think I blew him off. I have to talk to him.* He guessed his phone was still in his jacket pocket, but that Jordan would not let him call John in peace.

"Aren't you going to ask what happened?" she asked.

Brian looked at her puzzled.

Jordan looked a little hurt that he didn't remember. "My big meeting? I had to leave here and give my presentation and come back. It was crazy."

"You know. Before we get into that, I'd like a soda."

"Of course, babe. There's a vending machine in the cafeteria. I'll be right back."

Brian slipped off the bed and stood up on shaky legs. *I can do this.* He took a step towards his jacket, only to feel a sharp pain of the needle from his IV pull him back. He moved the IV drip stand a few feet and grabbed his phone. It was just where he thought it would be.

John's number was at the top of his recent calls list. He hesitated for a second. Took a deep breath. The phone rang a few times before he heard his voice.

"Hello?" He sounded groggy. Brian checked the time on his phone and realized that it was a little after 8 in the morning. Shit.

"Hi, John? It's Brian."

"Yes? Brian? Why are you calling?" John's voice was soothing. He felt that sense of home he had in his dream.

"I'm sorry. I can't see you tonight."

"That's OK. What's going on?"

"I'm in the hospital."

"What?" John said, sounding more awake.

"I went to a restaurant last night and woke up in the hospital. I'm not sure when they will let me out. Look, I'm sorry to miss out first meeting—."

"That's not important. Are you alright?"

"Yeah, I feel fine."

"Do the doctors know what happened?"

"What do doctors know? The important thing is that I'm feeling better and want to reschedule with you."

Brian sounded worried. "Why don't you wait until you get out of the hospital and give me a call…"

"No. Wait. How about we meet up next week" Brian took the silence on the other end of the phone to be encouraging. At least he wasn't saying no. "What about Monday?"

"I don't want you to hurt yourself."

"I'm good now, I swear."

"OK. Monday, same place, same time. But you will let me know if you feel even the slightest bit sick?"

"I promise." After Brian hung up, he felt light and excited.

Brian was concerned about work. He was in charge of an issue on the badly underserved and underappreciated police officers in America's urban centers. It needed to be put to be in less than two weeks. Now that he was editor, it was his responsibility to recruit talented writers and he gathered a good group. He was especially proud of his article on expanding police powers in inner-city neighborhoods. The others were equally as good. Some real personal stuff about a family whose daughter was killed by an immigrant. Another about how Black Lives Matter was creating an atmosphere that causes police injuries and death. He felt that it was going to be a strong first issue for the new year. He was anxious to get back to work.

When he checked his mail, there were a bunch of messages. He fought the pain of a migraine as he read through his unopened email. Some people had pressing questions, others told him not to worry and that everything was under control. Stan told him the truth—things were OK, but they weren't going to be if he was out too long. Just as he got started answering his emails, Jordan came back with a generic lemon-lime soda from the hospital vending machine.

"What's the matter with you?" she said as she took the phone out of his hands and gave him a kiss on the forehead. He gave it up without a fight. She took her post beside his bed.

"I was about to tell you about my presentation before I went to get the soda. Well, the presentation went well. I think we landed that client. I used your idea…"

Brian didn't hear the end of her sentence. He drifted off despite fighting to stay awake. He dreamt of work. Everyone at the magazine was mad at him. Every time he tried to talk to someone, they turned their back to him. Suddenly, he was standing on a street corner with his coat and gloves on, but he wasn't cold. There was a dog sitting beside him. Then, he was sitting on the corner too in the exact same position as the dog. When he woke up, he was curled in a ball on the bed and a small group of doctors were standing above him.

"Don't mind us, we're just finishing up rounds," said the oldest, and Brian assumed most senior, doctor. "Mr. Eppler, it looks like you're going home today. We can't find anything wrong with you. We did every kind of test imaginable and you're clear."

"Wait, that's it? 'I'm clear.' Can't you tell me something about what happened? I don't want it to happen again."

"Don't worry, Mr. Eppler. If you experience the same symptoms, just come back and we'll take care of you. In the meantime, take a few days off. It was probably from exhaustion."

Jordan insisted that he take a three-day weekend. You have got to rest. You heard the doctors; they think you're exhausted and I do too.

"OK. But I go back to work on Monday," Brian said.

He didn't think that there was much he could do but rest. His limbs felt like they were made of sand. He was dizzy and achy. Jordan thought he had the flu, but he didn't have a fever. Brian was sleeping at weird times of the day. He found himself just up from a nap at 2 in the afternoon. *Maybe I can get something done while Jordan is at work,* he thought. He went to his laptop and opened the file for the latest issue. He was nauseous, and sweating and his hands were clammy. He decided that he wasn't fit to work yet. Brian closed the work file.

I'm already in front of the computer, he thought. He had the apartment to himself. He thought he earned a little alone time. He typed in 'porn' and a cascade of websites filled his screen. He was used to sneaking around to watch porn. Jordan once found him masturbating to a website and she berated him with questions for two days about why he found the women in the films more attractive than her. He clicked on a link that opened to a man giving another man a blow job. "That's not what I wanted," he said. He wasn't gay. He never had so much as a thought about another man. In school, when his friends were getting blown or hand jobs from gay guys, he would rather get it from the school slut, Tammy Bear. He smiled to himself. He hadn't thought of her in a long time. He heard that she got her life together and was working in a women's domestic violence shelter somewhere.

He closed that page and opened another link. This time, it was a caption that read, "Monster Cock Gangbang." Before he could stop himself, he opened the link. There were three buff white guys taking turns fucking a skinny one on all fours. One fucked his ass, the other stuffed his dick down his throat and the third one waited his turn while the skinny one stroked his dick. He tried to shut off the computer or turn his head away, but he couldn't do either. He was fixed in front of the screen, watching the men grunt and moan. Brian's breath quickened. He was drawn to the face of the man getting fucked. His eyes were closed. He eagerly swallowed the dick of the men who thrust themselves into his mouth. Brian bit his lip hard to stop himself from getting hard. Soon, he strained against his pajama pants. He reached inside his underwear and began to stroke himself. The guy being fucked in the movie was now on his back with his legs in the air. There was one man pushing inside him, while the other two knelt on the bed beside his head, each taking turns making him suck their dicks. Brian stroked faster, his attention focused on the sight of the man's dick in and out of the skinny one's asshole and his tongue eagerly licking the dicks in his face. He closed his eyes and he was kneeling in front of John.

John was long and thick and uncut. Licking his erect shaft from the balls to the tip and then swallowing as much as he could, Brian moaned with pleasure. John pushed his dick deeper down his throat and Brian started to gag. When he came up for air, John ordered him on his back and positioned himself above him. He could taste the salt of John's dick on his lips. He eagerly put his legs in the air and waited for the feeling of John's dick inside his ass. John's face hovered above his. His delicate features contrasted with the burning fullness of the large dick inside him. He wiggled his hips to maneuver John's dick as deep inside of him as he could. He whispered, "Deeper. Faster," and John obliged, pounding his body, filling his ass. John smiled, pleased with Brian's responses and leaned in to kiss him on the lips.

Still sitting in front of the computer screen, Brian was only vaguely aware that he was grunting. He licked his lips in anticipation of John's kiss when he heard Jordan's ringtone on his phone. He tried to ignore it, but the fantasy was rapidly disintegrating in his mind. Shit! I'm so close. He rubbed furiously for a few more seconds until he gave up and answered the phone.

"What?" Brian answered, annoyed.

"I just called to see if you're OK," Jordan said.

"I'm sorry. You woke me up from a nap. I guess I'm a little cranky."

"I'll say. Don't worry. I won't make this mistake, again. See you at dinner. You want anything?"

"I'm sorry, Jordan. I didn't mean to—"

"No. It's fine. See you later. Call me if you need something."

She hung up. Brian felt terrible and frustrated. He knew he wasn't actually having an affair, but it was beginning to feel like cheating on Jordan and he didn't even get to have his orgasm. *This is unhealthy,* he thought. *I'll meet with John on Monday, but I'll just tell him I can't do the project. There. Problem solved. Maybe I should lay down,* he thought. *This illness is doing weird things to me.* He went back to bed and got underneath the covers.

He didn't dream, or he didn't remember any dreams if he had them. He was woken up by the sound of the key turning in the lock. He opened his eyes, and it was dark out. *I must have been out for hours,* he thought. He called out, "Jordan! I'm in the bedroom." In the doorway was the waiter from the restaurant holding a paper bag and wearing a worried look on his face.

"You are calling me your ex-girlfriend's name again," he said. He looked like he was contemplating calling an ambulance. Brian looked around and everything else in the room was exactly as it was when he went to sleep. On his shirt was a name tag.

"La'Quan." He said the name out loud.

"Yes, baby, I'm here." La'Quan sat on the bed and put his hand on Brian's forehead. "You don't have a temperature, thank God. Well, I have some food from the restaurant. Are you hungry?"

Before he could answer, he heard a key in the door. He turned to see who was coming in. Jordan walked through the door. La'Quan was no longer in the apartment. His heart was pounding. He reached out to Jordan. "I think I was dreaming. Or maybe it was a hallucination."

"What? What did you see?" Jordan looked scared for him.

Brian was filled with shame. He could not tell her that he was hallucinating a Black gay lover. Shame washed over him and pain jabbed him in the gut. He wanted to lay down. "I just need to rest," he said, sitting on the couch.

"I'll make you some tea," Jordan said, dropping her things and rushing to the kitchen.

In his apartment on the other side of town, John blew out a candle and Brian fell into a fitful sleep.

Brian woke up but didn't remember his dream. It was the middle of the night and Jordan was asleep beside him. All he wanted was a shower. He gathered up fresh clothes, went to the bathroom, and let the hot water run until the bathroom was filled with steam. Brian stepped into the shower and let the hot water flow over his body. He closed his eyes and used Jordan's bath sponge to wash with a sudsy, sweet smelling lather.

As he ran the sponge over his arms, he felt arms wrap around his waist and strong, open hands moved up from his stomach to his chest from behind him. He heard John's voice say, "We haven't done this in a long time." He felt John's face rest on his back. Brian dropped the sponge and wrapped John's arms closer around him. After a while, he moved John's arms from around his waist and then maneuvered around the tub to a squatting position behind John. John placed his hands flat on the wall as the water continued to stream down their bodies. Brian kissed the outside of John's ass, parting his brown cheeks carefully, then eagerly licked between them. Brian lost himself in the tang on his tongue and the smell of his own breath as he ate John's ass. John turned around and guided his dick into Brian's mouth. Brian stroked himself while he worked. The deeper John pushed himself down Brian's throat, the more Brian relaxed into his submission, until John strained to climax.

Brian heard someone rattling the doorknob and banging on the door. He stood up and opened the curtain to see La'Quan's barely breathing body on the bathroom floor. La'Quan was bloodied and his face was swollen from a horrible beating. Brian involuntarily dropped to his knees in the shower, eyes shut against the image of La Quan, but also to the force of pleasure that swept through his body like a bursting dam.

When Brian opened his eyes again, he was alone in the bathroom on his hands and knees having an orgasm so strong, it was painful. Jiz made its way down the drain.

"What's going on? I heard the most unearthly noise." Jordan was standing in the doorway with a horrified look on her face that Brian had never seen before.

She shut off the water and helped him out of the shower. Brian looked all around for La'Quan, but he was alone with Jordan in the bathroom.

"Look at your skin! How long have you been in here? I've been pounding on the door for 40 minutes. Thank God I figured out how to jimmy the door open." Her voice was close to panic, as she wiped him off with a towel.

With the door open, the steam was dissipating from the room. Brian caught a glimpse of himself in the bathroom mirror. His brown hair was hanging down below his ears and almost covering his eyes. His eyes were red. Jordan helped him into his underwear and a fresh pair of pajamas. Brian felt two things: the profound loss of John, which was like having his skin stripped away, and a cold fear of La'Quan. Not La'Quan himself, but it was as if La'Quan was the key to something terrifying.

Twenty minutes after Jordan helped him from the shower into bed, Brian's hard-on came back. In Brian's head was La'Quan's swollen eyes, bloodied face. Blood was trickling out of his ears as his body was being kicked by unknown assailants. The need to fuck roared in Brian like a storm. He rolled over and kissed Jordan awake.

"It's been so long," he said.

Jordan moaned in agreement and opened her pajama top. He brushed his tongue across her nipple and pulled down her underwear. At first, he thought he had drowned out the images of La'Quan with the feeling of being surrounded by her wetness. Jordan moved against him, eager to come. Then, the more he sunk into her body, emersed in her need and pleasure, the more he began to lose his desire. He felt himself retreat from her.

Brian switched their positions, putting her on top and then to the side, but he was still struggling to maintain a semi.

He flipped back on top of Jordan and allowed the image of La 'Quan's bloody face to slip back into his mind. He closed his eyes and exploded with a fierceness. When he opened his eyes, Jordan pulled away from him, quickly running into the bathroom and locking the door.

"What?" he asked.

Jordan stayed locked in the bathroom. All she would say was, "Everything's fine. Give me a minute." When she finally emerged from the bathroom, she continued to deny anything was wrong. "It was nothing. You just looked so intense. You startled me. That's all," she said.

But Brian knew it was not fine. He felt that their relationship had turned a corner and neither of them would be the same. He was shaking. *What if she saw it? The real me?*

John sensed Brian's confusion and did not want to risk him becoming too distraught. He'd learned the hard way that people can overthink their desires, sometimes to the point of harming themselves. He blew softly into the cup of hot water and hummed a soft tune, knowing that it would soothe Brian's confusion and help him focus on the anticipation of seeing him again.

John sighed. *This was his calling, right? He was righting the wrongs of the universe.* John knew it was not his job to mete out justice. He had seen too many horrible things. He had seen too many beatings, rapes, mutilations, violations of the young, the old, the infirm, people who could not defend themselves, people who were overpowered, people who were surprised, people who were defeated or helpless or hopeless. John had seen enough, but he was created for one thing, to bring mercy to those who are crossing over. He didn't have bosses like the humans did. He did have something that the humans did not have—a singleness of purpose, a reason for being, an innate understanding of his place in the cosmos. It was up to him to watch and act. It was not his job to hand down judgment or meet out justice or deliver vengeance. His sole purpose was to give mercy to those in need and deserving of mercy. Could he have free will too? Could he step out of his role and reinterpret what mercy was? There was room for creativity in his work. The humans still had free will, but he could alter perceptions, interact with humans, guide them in different directions. And over the millennia, John had crafted ways to steer humans to a more merciful outcome.

He could only manipulate those judged for some mistake or transgression; he could not give them deliverance. But he could make their lives or final punishments less painful. Usually, that meant on the other side mercy would be granted. And after whatever actions the humans had taken, if it was determined that they deserved mercy, their punishments on the other side would not be as severe.

It occurred to him one day long ago that he could administer mercy on the human side of the veil, that there were no restrictions on when mercy had to come. That would it mean that their punishments on the other side would stay the same, but their lives as they lived them would take on more favorable attributes. John loved his work now that he had figured out that flexibility. It did not come in a flash but over time. He wasn't given a job description, orientation, a rule book, or any of the things humans have when they step into a particular job. But he had an internal compass and hard limitations to what he could and could not do. If it were up to John, he could stop the humans from engaging in their most egregious actions, the things that brought them judgment in the first place. He wished he could relieve the suffering by erasing events from the timeline. He wished he could manipulate the world such that there would be no more pain or violence, but humans still had free will, and this was at least something.

The subject line said, "Does a Black Man Suddenly Have a Hold on You?" Brian didn't recognize the sender. He almost deleted it, but the way it was worded made him curious. He clicked on it, half expecting it to be an offer from a prince or a colorful banner that he had just won $10,000 worth of merchandise if he bought some household items. Instead, there was a message:

Have you met a mysterious black man recently? Caramel brown skin, brown eyes, thin around 5'5"? If this is true, then meet me at The Ranch café, tomorrow 6pm. Do NOT tell him about this.

The person didn't sign it. Brian's heart pounded. *It couldn't be. John?* He backed away from the desk.

Stan waved at him from the other side of the office. "It's time for the meeting, buddy." Stan didn't look like his regular happy self. Brian followed him into the conference room. Brian knew he was being pulled in to get a talking to. He had not been able to work since the night at the restaurant. Every time he looked at his work, he got an splitting headache and intense nausea. *I will probably be fired soon,* he thought. He was surprisingly calm. For several days, he had been planning the severance package he could ask for given the magazine's current financial circumstances. Which he contemplated while he was supposed to be working.

The senior editors were waiting for him in the conference room.

"Brian," smiled his-least favorite senior editor. "You know we really value your hard work here. In just a short time you have shown tremendous promise as a writer and editor. We are concerned that you haven't fully recovered from your illness. Perhaps it would be better if you took an extended leave."

Brian knew he should feel terrible, but he didn't. He felt relieved. *Now, I can spend more time with John,* he thought.

Brian and John walked through one the few bookstores left in the city. It was Brian's idea to go to bookstores to look at other graphic novels in anticipation of their work together. Brian could not remember when he felt more content.

John lingered at a magazine rack. "Isn't this the magazine you work for?" He asked. The cover photo was of a group of Mexican men in handcuffs being guarded by border patrol agents. The headline read, "Are You Safe?" This was the first issue of the magazine that Brian personally managed from start to finish.

For the first time, Brian was ashamed of his work. He did not want John to see the other articles calling for the end of Medicaid and Affirmative Action. A creeping sense of dread ran through his body. The pounding headache and nausea that plagued him since that night at the restaurant returned with a vengeance.

John put his hand casually on Brian's shoulder. "Are you OK?" He asked.

Brian tried to smile, "I'm fine," he said, steering John away from the magazine rack. "Let me show you one of my favorite books. I love this Phillip K. Dick", he said, holding a copy of *The Man in the High Castle.*

John touched Brian on the small of his back while they both looked at the cover of the science fiction novel. The pain and nausea subsided, and Brian tried not to move, so as to savor the moment. The longer John touched him, the harder he was becoming. Eventually, he had to turn away and adjust himself. The sensation of John's touch lingered with him long after the two had parted ways, mounting his frustration.

At home, Brian waited impatiently for Jordan to go to sleep, so that he could masturbate, but she was up working on another presentation. Brian couldn't sleep. His skin was on fire. John was all he could think of. *What was he doing now? Was he thinking of me?* Brian paced in front of the large windows of his apartment in an effort to hide the stiffness in his pajamas from Jordan. He realized that she was looking at him nervously from the corner of her eyes. They hadn't had sex since that night she found him in the shower. He didn't want to and he got the feeling she was generally avoiding him. He went to the bathroom and used his phone to jack off to the *Fucked by a Thug* gay porn website he recently bought a subscription to. It was exclusively videos of white men being fucked by various Black men who were supposed to be "thugs," but he recognized some of them from other porn videos where they played other characters. After he came, he was hard again in seconds. All he could think of was John's hands on his body and face. He pushed away ugly images of La 'Quan that threatened to overtake his mind. The pacing helped keep them at bay. He noticed that Jordan was no longer working at her desk, but on the cell phone in the kitchen, whispering. The air smelled of lemons.

Brian looked out of the window onto the city streets and longed for air. He threw on some clothes and grabbed his coat, yelling, "I'm going for a walk," as he walked out the door. In the back of his mind, he thought Jordan was probably at her limit and ready to leave him. Once outside, he breathed a little better. With the night air cooling his skin, he felt calmer than he had in the apartment. His hard-on subsided. He didn't know how long he walked. He was gone long enough that he didn't think that Jordan would be there when he got back.

Brian found himself in the Central West End and lined up behind other patrons at the first club he saw that had an exclusively male crowd out front. It wasn't that he was looking for a gay bar, but once he found one, he felt pulled inside. He was sweating. Brian noticed that he was the only one with a coat. He took it off while still in line and realized that his outfit made him stand out. In his rush to leave, Brian grabbed the first thing that he saw available in the bedroom—a polo shirt and khaki pants. He slipped on his loafers that were sitting at the front door and put on his trench coat against the cold. He looked like he was going to a convention. Brian wanted to tell the men in line that it wasn't his fault that his clothes were not fit for the club, that he didn't plan on coming there, but that also sounded weird.

"Are you lost, sugar?" A Black man with flawless brown skin and bright yellow false eyelashes asked him in a southern drawl. The man was surrounded by friends, all Black, each one with flamboyant outfits.

"No...thank you," Brian said, taken aback.

The man and his friends laughed. He felt stupid. He wanted to leave the line, but he couldn't get his feet to move. Once inside the club, Brian felt even more out of place, with his coat over his arm. He was lost. He would have left except for his overwhelming, burning desire to be pushed to his knees.

Brian ordered a beer at the bar and looked around, hoping to run into John. A big white guy in a tight T-shirt that revealed his muscular chest and tight abs sat next to him at the bar. Brian tried not to look as frightened as he felt. The man looked directly at Brian, like he was a book that he was skimming. Brian tried to break the tension with a joke. "Do you know where the coat check is?" he said, holding up his coat. The man said nothing, but put his hand firmly on Brian's leg, which instantly made him hard again.

The man got up and Brian followed him. They moved through the thumping dance floor, weaving between the sweaty bodies, and down a narrow staircase. They landed in a dark, crowded room. The air was thick with the smell of sweat, lube, and shit. He couldn't see anyone very clearly, but he could hear the grunting in the dark. As the man in the T-shirt pushed his shoulders down, the taste of lemons, sweet and tangy at the same time, gathered in the back of his throat making him crest to the edge of exploding. The man forced his dick so far down Brian's throat so fast and so hard, he thought he was going to throw up. Pleasure almost overtook him, pushing squealing noises out from deep inside his gut up and out of his throat. Brian couldn't breathe, his lungs burned, and he was dizzy. He felt he could pass out either from not breathing or intense pleasure, they both threatened to take him over and melt into each other at the same time. The man came on his face and pushed him aside, making his way through the dark room alone. Brian didn't know what happened to him. He stood up, but before he could get his bearings, someone else pushed him face-first up against the wall and pulled down his pants. Brian didn't know what this man looked like, only that he was the same height and firm and commanding. He pressed Brian's forehead against the wall while he tried to push inside him. Brian felt a burning pain in his asshole.

"You're too tight. You didn't oil up for this? What are you, a virgin?" The man hissed at him in the dark. The man grunted with disapproval. There were gallon jugs of lube with a pump on top in various spots around the room. Brian looked over his shoulder enough to see a white hand in the dark put a few pumps of thick liquid into his hand. The man wiped the liquid on Brian's ass. Brian braced for the burning sensation to come. The man pushed himself into Brian's asshole. "Take it," he rasped. The lube didn't take the pain away, but it did make it possible for the man's dick to move deep inside him. Brian was willing to endure the pain just to feel the man's rough hands on him. Then, he felt the thump of the man's dick on his prostate. He was unprepared for the spike of electricity that ran from balls to his gut. Brian heard himself whisper, "Yes" and "Thank you," as if in prayer.

Brian came twice before the man was finished with him. He found that he was shaking as he tried to pull himself together to leave. Brian suddenly remembered his coat and felt around on the floor for it while he tried to pull up his pants. He couldn't find his coat, but he found lots of hands pulling his face into a stranger's crotch or sticking their fingers down his throat. Someone else put two fingers up his ass and he yelped like a puppy. He abandoned his coat and stumbled out of the back of the club into the crowded alley, still trying to button up his pants. The alley was lined with male couples kissing, smoking, and dancing. He made his way toward the street where his car was parked.

Someone in the line waiting to get in yelled, "I hope I have as good a time as that queen!" Brian realized that his clothes were disheveled, and his zipper was down. He wondered if people could see the cum on his face in the dimly lit alley.

At that moment, Brian saw, Stan and his girlfriend of the month, Jessica, walk out of a nearby restaurant. The three of them looked at each other for what felt like hours.

From behind him, he felt a hand on his shoulder. It was the beautiful, brown-skinned man with the yellow eyelashes. "Now, you had a good time tonight. Had some fun? But you know a good time's not free, right? You're a capitalist—you look like one. Everything costs. It's time to pay." The man pushed Brian forward and he stumbled past Stan and his girlfriend, without speaking to his car. He knew his time at the journal was over.

A tall blonde man walked into the café. He immediately looked at Brian, searching his face for confirmation. The two nodded at each other. The man was a little thicker than he expected. And older. He had on a plain gray T-shirt and jeans. *John wouldn't have anything to do with someone who looked like this. Too boring,* Brian thought.

"Hey, my name is Chris." The two shook hands.

"Brian."

Chris sat down and nervously looked around. "You didn't tell him about this did you? I mean, he's not here or anything?"

"I don't know who you are talking about. Look, I came here out of curiosity. My curiosity is sated. I'm going to go." Brian stood up to go.

"He'll never let you go, you know, Brian."

Brian sat down again.

"Hey, let's order something," Chris said, trying to break the heavy tension. He motioned for a waitress and ordered an herbal tea with lemon and Brian ordered coffee. The two avoided looking at each other for a moment, but the drinks came mercifully quickly.

"How did you find me?" Brian asked.

"I heard from a friend of a friend that there was a guy who used to be a conservative journalist who suddenly quit and disappeared. And I took a chance."

"That's it? Now I know you're crazy. There are plenty of guys like that."

Chris shook his head. "No, no, no. Not with that kind of rapid change of personality. I've been around a long time, and I haven't seen it happen that often. It happened to me too. Did he turn your life upside down and you don't know how?"

"How do I know we are talking about the same person?"

Chris smiled, but there wasn't any joy in it. He said, "I am sure of it. You are too. I contacted others with the same message, and you were among the few who responded. I don't know if that means the others were too scared, or all my emails went to spam, but only a few people would respond to that kind of crazy message."

Chris was encouraged by Brian's willingness to listen and continued, "I met this guy one day at a baseball game. Minor leagues, nothing special. We sat next to each other, and he caught the game ball and then he gave it to me. We started to chat, and I found out that he is a sports collector. I couldn't stop thinking about him. I went over to his house to see his collection and I didn't want to leave. I found myself thinking of him every day. Does any of this sound familiar?"

"My guy's a graphic artist. He doesn't sound like your person at all."

"Wait, let me finish. He was a stockbroker with one guy and a pharmacy rep with another. He changes what he does all the time. But it's always the same. We meet him and are inexplicably pulled to him, and then creepy stuff starts to happen."

"Creepy?"

"Like we start seeing things and remembering things…" Chris swallowed hard and could not Brian's eyes for a few moments, "Then, he does it." Chris paused to take a drink from his tea. The lemon filled the air. Chris rubbed his hands on his pants repetitively. "He won't stay with you, but he won't leave either. It's been ten years and I still think about him all the time. I meet other men, have boyfriends, but it doesn't last because I measure everyone up to him. I can't go back to women either. The men I really want, the ones who are most like him, don't want me." Brian could tell that Chris was on the verge of tears. "It's probably too late for you to leave but know that you're not alone. We have to be here for each other."

"What did this guy do? Did he swindle you out of money?"

"No. He never asked for money. That's what's so hard about it. He made me see myself clearly and now I'm stuck with it. "

"What if I tell him that you came here today? I bet he would be interested in this."

"Don't!" Chris pleaded, looking around again. "Please."

"What are you so afraid of?"

"That he'll talk to me again and I will go insane. The closer I am to him, the deeper I see within my own soul."

Brian felt sorry for him. He saw the terror in Chris' eyes. Brian could tell that whatever revelations he had were enough to make Chris want to run.

Brian left the café. He didn't want to be free. He wanted John to be with him, always. He could not believe the man he was talking about to be John. His John was too kind to do anything like that. Brian put Chris out of his mind. Whatever was haunting that poor man wasn't relevant to him. *It's not the same person*, he thought. *It couldn't be.* All he felt with John was love and desire.

Brian couldn't remember returning home, but he was there with John looking at him with a coldness that made him shake.

John spoke in voice that Brian didn't recognize, it was so deep and resonant that it was almost otherworldly. "They were wearing a pair of lemon-yellow pumps. Brand new. They usually never encountered a soul on their walk the block from the restaurant to the bus stop. But this night, this night, they encountered you. What happened?"

Brian started to talk despite himself. "Me and Buzz and Tommy and York, we were kicked out of Tommy's house for being loud while his mother was trying to sleep. We were drinking and high."

"Go on," John said, never taking his cold stare away.

Brian tried to keep himself from saying any more but found that he could not refuse John's command. "And there he was, moving at a fast clip to the bus stop." Brian took a deep breath and kept his eyes glued to the kitchen table. "I remember thinking, why should he have so much freedom? It made me angry. But I didn't throw the first punch," Brian said, finding the strength to look at John. "That was Tommy. Why don't you bother him? Punish him? He started it!"

"What did you do?"

Brian strained against the force of his body, compelling him to speak the truth. The answer came out of him in stuttering venom. "I kicked him. I saw that he had, like, small breasts or something. They weren't obvious under his shirt at first. The fighting must have torn his clothes. There they were—firm and full and straining against his shirt. I kicked them as hard as I could."

Brian felt drained. All he wanted was to crawl away, but a force be-yond his comprehension kept him from moving.

"We were just playing around," Brian tried pleading for John's un-derstanding. "I saw him come out of the restaurant before anyone else. He was walking in those yellow shoes, women's shoes, I guess I was staring at him, and the others followed where I was looking. It was fun-ny at first. I mean, we were just kidding around. We were just kids from the suburbs looking for something to do. We had gotten kicked out of Tommy's and then a club for having fake IDs so we had nowhere to go and we were restless. I don't know who yelled first, maybe it was me."

John cracked an icy smile. "You know exactly what you said. What was it?"

Brian didn't want to say, but the words would not stop. "I yelled, 'Hey, is that a boy or a girl?' Somebody else said, 'I think it's a faggot.' Then we all chimed in: 'Look at the Black faggot.' We all laughed. He didn't even glance our way. I don't know why, but things turned when my friend Jeff said, 'My dad says we might have to move because there are too many niggers moving into the neighborhood.' I remember be-ing shocked that he used that word. The next thing I knew, we were following him."

"Use his name. You know it. La'Quan," John said.

Brian felt like he was back on the dark street a couple of blocks away from the strip of restaurants near his childhood home. The fog was moving in, and it covered the street like gauze. The words spilled out of him. "I was kind of sick from the smell of lemons that was heavy in the air. It wasn't perfume. More like lemon squares. I wanted to throw up, but I didn't want to look weak in front of my friends, so I swal-lowed and joined the others. La'Quan turned around and said, 'Leave me the fuck alone. I'm just minding my own business.' Then, I said, 'I don't like having to see your Black faggot face in my neighborhood. I have a right not to have to see you.'"

Brian took a deep breath. "La'Quan didn't back down. He cursed at us and yelled at us to stay back, but things got out of hand, and we moved closer to him." Brian closed his eyes, and he remembered his own younger voice. "I said, 'What are you going to do about it? What, faggot? Got nothing to say?' La'Quan hit one of the guys in the face, bloodying his lip. Tommy threw the first punch. He hit La'Quan in the stomach, making him double over in pain. Someone else kicked the back of his knees, sending him to the ground. We took turns kicking him. I remember the smell of lemons in the air and La'Quan was throwing up yellow liquid and I punched him in the face while he was on the ground. Then, I noticed a car go by, but no one stopped. When I looked back, I saw his name tag for the first time. I remembered that name, La'Quan, because it was unusual." Brian paused for a moment and said, "His face was so bloody and swollen."

Brian was fidgeting in his chair, unable to open his eyes. He knew that John was still looking at him in a way that made him want to scream, but he kept talking, "We got scared when we heard a police siren. Everybody went separate ways, and I took off down the private alley behind some of the houses. When I stopped to breathe, I noticed that my hands were scarred from punching. And—"

"Say it!" John's yell ripped through Brian's very being.

Brian did not want to say the next thing. He struggled to keep silent, but John's voice was a loud echo in his head that threatened to crack open his skull if he didn't obey. He felt that he would rather die than say the next thing out loud, but he could not stop. "And I had massive hard-on straining in my pants," he said, his voice shaking. "I went to my girlfriend's house so we could have sex."

When he opened his eyes, he was still sitting at the kitchen table. John was across from him. John was silent, but his eyes locked into Brian's soul.

"How did you know?" Brian asked.

John kept his gaze on him in silence.

"Are you going to kill me?" Brian asked.

"No." John sucked his teeth. "To think I'd waste my time killing your pathetic—. No. I'm not going to kill you. That would be too easy." John slapped his hand on the table. "Finish the story," he demanded.

Brian looked down at the table. "I saw him, and he looked so free. Like he was totally comfortable being that. Everyone in my world knew it was wrong, that it was disgusting. They were so sure about it. You know?" Brian looked in search of some sympathy from John but was confronted by an emotionless harshness that he had feared would be there when he found out how ugly he really was. "You, you know what high school is like, right? La'Quan wasn't supposed to be happy. He was supposed to be miserable and afraid. He was supposed to take everything he ever felt and stuff it down inside and never look at it again, never show it to anybody. Instead, he was flaunting it where anyone could see."

Brian reached out to hold John's hand. He just wanted to touch him. He would feel better if he just got a chance to touch him, but John pulled away. "I...I was young, you know. Stupid. I would never do anything like that now. Don't look at me like that. Tell me what you're thinking. I love—"

John put his hand up before Brian could finish his sentence. "Here is what's going to happen. I will grant you mercy. You will not go back to your old life."

"Jordan? She didn't do anything. Please don't punish her. She loves me and I've been an ass to her. She's completely innocent."

"Is she? Did she agree with you in all your bigotry? What about at her workplace? In casual interactions with people on the street? What did she do?" Brian didn't say anything.

"What will happen to me? I will do anything, just please don't leave."

"Oh, don't worry. I will never leave your heart. I will sit there like a popular tune running in the back of your mind that you can't get rid of. There will be other men who remind you of me, but you will never have them. As a matter of fact, you will never have a Black man in your life, but that's all you will ever crave."

"That's your version of mercy? I will never have sex again?"

"If that's what you choose. You can sleep with anyone you want, except the men that you want the most."

"And women?"

John shook his head.

"You will continue to be made unbearably ill by anything that is remotely prejudiced, bigoted, racist, homophobic, transphobic, xenophobic..., etc. You will get no pleasure out of hurting others emotionally or physically. In other words, I am gifting you with a kinder life."

Brian began to cry.

John rolled his eyes. "Long ago I grew tired of human execration, enmity, and wickedness. I stopped and I decided to do something about it. I cannot prevent major events either personal or historical. I am sent to show transgressors the goodness of mercy, to show them another way."

"You were sent here to judge and punish me?" Brian said, sniffling.

"You have already been judged. Punishment is someone else's work. I can only show you mercy and reveal another path."

"This is cruel."

"Oh no! No, no, no, no, no. Cruel is beating a young man almost to death and leaving him to die on a cold street corner. Cruel is shutting your eyes to others' suffering and being determined to stoke the flames of hatred that you know will bring more suffering. This…" John tapped the table for emphasis. "This is mercy."

John began to disappear right before his eyes. Brian sat, not knowing what to do, blinking as his vision shifted. Later, Brian woke up in bed, soaking in a cold sweat.

As the days passed, Brian's world grew smaller without his heart's desire. Watching Black performers made him ache for actual contact. Nothing he did or said made a difference. He could never rise above casual contact with Black men or women. Eventually, Black people did not see him. They moved out of the way, realizing someone was there, but they didn't engage or talk to him. Brian slowly faded away.

ANGEL

OF

LIGHT

2023

"...there are evil men in the world, truly evil men. Sometimes we hear of them, but more often they work in absolute darkness."

Stephen King, *Salem's Lot*

I am going to tell you about the last time I saw my first love and friend, Keith. The details of my visit with him have slowly returned after many months of fog and shame.

After 5 years of radio silence, Keith, sent me a text. It was simply, "Come visit me," along with a West Hollywood address. I tried calling him back, but he never answered. He wasn't on any social media sites that I could find. Even his Adam for Adam profile was seriously neglected. Keith had been using the handle DRKASSNITE21 on various sites since he was 21. We were both turning 40. His picture was gone, and he had taken down his personal statement and description, and there was nothing about his covid or mpox status. All it said was last tested for HIV in 2015 and was looking for fun. "Fun," I assumed meant sex and drugs, although, last I heard, he was trying to get clean.

Keith and I met in college when I had long hair, breasts, and a girl's name. He recognized who I was even before I did and called me "little brother" even though we were the same age. I had a huge crush on him from the moment I saw him. He was tall and dark-skinned, with the most gorgeous smile I had ever seen. He had the kind of smile that made it impossible to be mad at him for long. I would start off the evening angry at his eternal lateness or that he stood me up for the third time in a row, and all he would have to do is flash me that incredible smile and I melted like a frozen stream during a spring thaw.

We lost touch and then finally, finally we found ourselves in the same area. He was in Los Angeles, and I was in Santa Barbara. I came to visit him every weekend. By that time, I had chosen the name Richard, after my grandfather, and had been out as a bisexual man for many years. He happened to catch me at a time when I was single. He was in an open relationship with this white guy. I didn't like his boyfriend. He wanted to rule over Keith, but Keith saw him as just wanting to take care of him. Keith had a rough childhood with parents that were too busy with their careers to pay much attention to him. He pretty much raised himself. Keith was always looking for that man who would make him feel safe and taken care of. We saw each other for a few months. Maybe it's too much to call him an ex because we were never really in a relationship but we have always been friends. Sex was very good. I enjoyed his body and I want to believe he enjoyed mine.

"I'm a top," I told him the first time we slept together.

"I'm verse," he said, but I knew that was a lie. Every story he ever told me was about his adventures as a top. I didn't say anything. I knew he was being open to make me comfortable. I loved him even more in that moment.

We parted on a bad note. I heard his boyfriend talking to him like he was a child. He said to Keith, "Who else would have you but me? If you would listen to me, you wouldn't be so miserable right now like the rest of those people you're friends with."

I was one of "those people." I told him to dump that white boy. He told me to go home. A mutual friend of ours said that they saw Keith two years later living in Dallas in his mother's house, having just come out of rehab. I was happy to hear that. I didn't follow up. I didn't think he wanted to see me. Besides, I was all wrapped up in this 25-year-old guy I was dating who was all wrapped up in me being his sugar daddy.

When I got Keith's text my role as sugar daddy had fallen apart some time earlier, and I spent the previous year trying to deal with my drinking. I had been drinking all the time, going to parties, hooking up with random people and attempting not to think about how lonely I was. I decided I was too young to quit drinking altogether and tried moderation. I was still lonely, but at least I wasn't so dead inside. I was really happy to see his text. Secretly, I hoped it meant that Keith and I could start again and, this time, do it right.

I knew from the second I saw the house that Keith was shacked up with some other white man, probably much older than him. The house was beautiful on the outside. A monument to old West Hollywood. It was on a street lined with large oak trees, with an immaculate lawn that was next to other immaculate lawns in front of other old houses. Each house was set back from the sidewalk, had large windows and fenced backyards. There were no McMansions on that block. Everything looked like it was out of the film *Sunset Boulevard*. Like the other houses, it had a large front door. This one was red and unusually wide. There were two big windows on the second floor made of stained glass, which despite their bright coloring and the sunshine, were dark and grey. The way the windows sat above either side of the front door, it seemed from the sidewalk that the house was looking at me with a wide grin—no grimace. I couldn't decide if the house was laughing at me or sneering. Either way, my blood ran cold suddenly, and for a split second, I thought of turning back to my car.

The closer I got to the house, the harder my heart started to beat. I chalked this up to being nervous about seeing Keith again. Would he still be mad at me for telling him to leave his last boyfriend? Would this boyfriend be any better? I rang the bell and the moment the door opened, I felt a sense of calm, not like comfort, but almost sedation. My heartbeat slowed and I felt as if I couldn't get upset if I tried. Standing in the doorway was a 60-ish white man, medium build, average height. He wasn't particularly handsome, but not ugly either, obviously wealthy but understated in his Brioni shirt and Ferragamo sandals—just the type that Keith liked. I was suddenly very aware of my H&M T-shirt and twill pants. I felt cheap and boring.

"Hi. My name is Buddy. You must be Richard. I've heard so many great things about you." He was tan and full of energy. He had a broad smile and perfect teeth.

"Nice to meet you," I smiled and looked around for Keith, as I stepped into the grand entrance hall. It was all there. The marble staircase, the granite inlay tables. I wasn't an art major in college, but I took a contemporary queer art class one semester, so I recognized the male nudes of Robert Mapplethorpe, Rotimi Fani Kayode and David Hockney hanging in the foyer. Buddy led me into the living room. It definitely looked like we stepped into another time. The room was huge. All the furniture was classic art deco style, with its plush velvet chairs, couches and settees framed by dark wood, matching dark wood tables, with legs that curled at the bottom. It even had a Steinway grand piano. A beautiful Black man stared at us from the painting, framed in flowers. The Kehinde Wiley painting hung on the wall and pulled the room together. The thick velvet red curtains canceled all light from the windows but gave the room a rich, mesmerizing glow in the recessed lighting.

Keith sat on one of the two gold velvet couches, in what was probably Buddy's J. Crew hand-me-downs—a Polo shirt and Bermuda shorts. He was so thin, the clothes hung on him like a hanger. He looked like some preppy reject. I wanted to get Keith alone to find out why he looked so ragged, but Buddy didn't look like he was going anywhere soon.

"Would you like a drink?" Buddy asked. I made a pact with myself to only have two drinks a day. I had been doing well with that promise for weeks and felt comfortable accepting his offer, confident that I would have only one more before going to sleep.

One turned into 3, turned into 5. Then I stopped counting. I remember talking a lot about my work. Buddy called me "a gentleman and a scholar," and said, "What a rare treat to have a member of the professoriate here with us."

I remember laughing at the stilted way he talked. "You sound like someone from another time."

"I guess I am for you young people," he laughed and clapped me on the back.

The last thing I remember of that night was feeling a hand across my chest. I woke up fully clothed in a fairly large guest room, with a four-poster bed and velvet eggplant-colored curtains. I had a slight headache, and the room spun a little, but given how much I drank, I expected much worse. I put on fresh clothes and then realized the door was wide open. I stepped out into the hall and found my way downstairs. Buddy was at the foot of the stairs and waved me out onto the enclosed porch.

Breakfast was already starting with a large spread of pancakes, sausage, bacon, eggs of various kinds, biscuits, and coffee. I started with black coffee.

Keith and Buddy were slowly making their way through the selection of food. I wondered where all the food came from. Had they cooked all this? Did Buddy have it catered? I decided to start off the conversation with something easy.

"Buddy, what do you do? Keith didn't tell me anything."

"I'm not surprised. He's been so sequestered lately." He continued to talk before I could ask what he meant by "sequestered". "I run a philanthropic organization. I decided to put my family funds to work for others." He paused as if he was used to praise or applause. I just waited for him to inevitably continue to talk about himself, "The Angel of Light charity seeks to give the unhoused and those who suffer from food insecurity a second chance. We realize that the politicians in the city really don't care about the homeless population and only mention them when it's time to get re-elected. We care 24 hours a day, 365 days a year, and it doesn't matter if it's an election year or not.

"The charity is a jewel in the crown, so to speak, of my family's philanthropic legacy. They have other business ventures associated with our name, of course, but this is the thing that I am most proud of and what I am most dedicated to. Many of the people who come to our charity suffer from addiction. You know, before the opioid crisis hit white America, many of the city's Black men were being rounded up and incarcerated for their illnesses. I pride myself on trying to put a stop to that practice by backing certain progressive politicians, but even more so by taking in a few people here and there who I thought were vulnerable to the prison system and we're going to get lost and fall through the cracks."

Everything about his boasting about his "philanthropic legacy" made me ill. I resisted rolling my eyes, but I couldn't stop myself from pointing out the obvious. "Angel of Light?" I asked, "That's a strange name for a charity."

"Oh really, why? We want to shine a light on the dark corners of the city and show people a way out."

"I say that, only because I thought Satan was the angel of light in the Bible."

He laughed, "You're probably right. I'm not one for church, although I do partner with some of the city's most influential and prominent Black ministers. It's funny that they never pointed that out."

Keith seemed distant and drained, like he had fallen into a deep well. I was determined to drag him out of his despair, but I needed to get him away from Buddy to do it.

Buddy was unphased by my crack about the name of his charity.

"Despite this coincidence, we are a legitimate charity. We take men who society has thrown away and we bring them into the fold. We help them make something of their lives and they in turn have meaningful work. Everyone wins."

"Meaningful work?" I asked. Keith gave me a warning look.

"Yes, we put them to work at the organization, mostly, but it's better than skid row."

I couldn't tell if Buddy was pretending, but the longer he talked about the Angels of Light philanthropy, the more energized he became.

"Where are my manners," he beamed, "Will you join us for breakfast?" Buddy gestured to the buffet of choices before us. He was standing in front of the couch, smiling, friendly. He put his hand out to help me up. "You look a little tired. I hope you're not coming down with something."

He was right about me coming down with something. I suddenly felt achy and flushed, as if I was getting the flu. I panicked for a second, thinking that I may have picked up Covid before coming down to Los Angeles. I tried to continue the conversation, determined to see if my instincts about Buddy were real.

"You talk about these men as if you own them," I said and then immediately regretted it. I didn't want Keith to throw me out as he did with the last boyfriend I confronted. But Keith kept eating, methodically going from his food to sips of coffee. He was dipping pieces of toast in runny egg yolks and chewing on bacon. None of it looked appetizing. The question crossed my mind, *Had I eaten since I got here?* I couldn't remember. I was not hungry even though I didn't think I had anything other than alcohol since I arrived the day before. *Maybe it really is the flu,* I thought.

I was surprised when Buddy laughed at what I said about owning the men. He didn't seem angry at all. Keith's mood changed as well. He was no longer distant or flashing me warning looks, but buoyant, matching Buddy's upbeat disposition.

"Keith said you were a good man. I can see why he likes you so much," he touched Keith's hand and in response, Keith flashed me a grin that looked nothing like the smile I knew so intimately and had come to miss in my life. Buddy held up his coffee cup as if to toast me. "Good. We need people to look out for those who cannot fight for themselves. If you weren't already employed, I would ask you to join my staff."

I glanced at Keith, who winked at me and smiled. I didn't know what to make of his response or Keith's look of approval. I went to put a piece of toast on my plate, but when I looked at the table, and for a flash, I saw maggots crawling over the white tablecloth on the food. I jumped up, nearly tripping on the metal chairs. Keith and Buddy looked at me with some concern.

"Are you OK?" Keith asked me.

When I looked back at the table, though, everything was back to normal.

"Maybe I'm too hungover to eat," I said as my stomach lurched. Keith got up to see if I was alright.

"That's understandable," Buddy said. "That used to happen frequently to me when I drank a little too much as a younger man. I can't afford such indulgences at my age." Buddy laughed, without getting up.

They continued to eat in the enclosed porch off a small sitting room toward the back of the house. I looked around to avoid the food. The porch was surrounded by brightly colored stain glass windows depicting calming landscapes. Large plants made the space even more inviting and wholesome.

"What kind of plants are these?" I asked.

Buddy and Keith finally stopped eating, and I stayed back to enjoy the light coming through the windows when I noticed it. A face at the top of the glass. I walked over to get a closer look, but it was too high up to see clearly. I dragged one of the heavy metal chairs to the corner where the face sat close to the ceiling. I stood on the chair and pulled out my phone. I took a picture of the figure and enlarged it on my phone. It was the house. The house where I was standing was painted into the glass design. It sat in a landscape that otherwise had no buildings, its face sprawled in the mocking grin I saw when I arrived. I almost fell off the chair. I heard Keith calling me to join them in the adjacent sitting room. When I looked back at the window, it seemed more like an ordinary house. *My imagination is getting the best of me,* I concluded.

After breakfast, we went back into the living room. Keith and Buddy were sitting across the room from each other. I sat on the couch next to Keith. "I saw the house in the stained glass on the porch," I said to Keith.

Buddy replied, "Oh yes. That was a long time ago, of course. The artist did a wonderful job capturing the soul of the house in such delicate detail. Don't you agree?"

"It's very detailed. I was almost expecting to see little versions of us inside the windows."

Buddy laughed so hard he snorted, but it sounded almost like a growl.

A headache creeped between my temples. "Maybe I should go lay down for a few minutes," I said. When I stepped onto the staircase,

I thought I saw an entirely different entryway. The grandeur was gone, and the floors and walls were grimy and had large holes or stripped spots. Cobwebs hung down from the ceiling. In a flash, it was back to the way it was. I ran back to my room and closed the door. I took off my clothes and crawled into bed.

I woke up some time later feeling better than when I went to bed. The door was cracked but I was almost certain I had closed it behind me. I resolved to push a chair under the doorknob the next time I went to bed.

I found Keith and Buddy in the living room like they hadn't moved since I went up for a nap.

"Welcome back!" Buddy was as ebullient as ever. Keith was looking more like himself, reserved and sweet.

Buddy insisted on taking me for a tour. The house was simple: bedrooms and Buddy's office upstairs, grand living room downstairs, and kitchen and the rooms for the men who were in Angels of Light downstairs through a door to what Buddy called the "Lost Wing."

"Why is it lost?"

"I have just never renovated it, is all. I don't show it because it's not as lovely as the rest of the house."

"I have a room down there," Keith said. For the first time, it seemed that Keith said something that Buddy didn't expect or approve of. He looked at him sharply, barely containing his rage.

"Darling, you would have your friend think I keep you separate from me. Of course, we share a bedroom," Buddy said through his teeth. Keith looked lost and distant again.

"Can I see it? I promise not to judge."

"Of course, you can, but another time," Buddy said ushering us back into the living room. He served drinks and I realized I didn't know what time it was. I hadn't seen my phone since I arrived. I couldn't find any clocks.

I asked Buddy again about the so-called "lost wing" of the mansion.

"Basically," he said, "this house is so big, and it was just me here, so I felt that it was too much for one person and a dedicated part of the house to be used for people who need temporary housing and a place to dry out—a stop on the way to making better choices."

The door to the lost wing was concealed behind the heavy red velvet curtain. *Leave it to gay men to give maximum drama,* I thought. Buddy and Keith excused themselves to take care of something and I was left alone downstairs.

Although, I knew I had no business going back there, but curiosity got the better of me and I went to move the curtain when I heard Buddy's voice, "It's time for cocktails!"

Ever since I was a kid when a grown-up said, "Don't touch that," I had to touch it. The thing would not leave my mind until I explored what was taboo about it. Drugs and alcohol were the same. I gravitated to them like a child's hand to a hot stove; I knew it was bad for me, but I just wanted to see what it was like. I paid heavily for it. I lost most of the people who ever loved me except my mother. That's it, siblings, cousins, friends. Everyone but Keith and my mother. Keith was my drinking and using buddy in college. I was always afraid of being caught with drugs, so I tended to use only with other people and never bought them myself. This caution was the result of seeing my cousin and uncle spend many years in and out of prison on drug charges—mostly for possession, sometimes for intent to distribute. I was terrified of being arrested and having to deal with the humiliation of the cops wondering what I am. How would they strip and cavity-search me? Would they call me names? Call me 'she'? Where would they put me? The women's prison? Or worse, with the men? Would I end up in solitary confinement for months or years?

Once, when I was 25 years old, I went to a house party in Brooklyn. I walked in and saw people drinking, doing lines of coke, smoking pot, dancing to music on the stereo system. I had to go to the bathroom, so as soon as I walked in the front door, I asked for directions to the bathroom. I was about to go back to the party, when I heard the police at the door responding to a noise complaint. Things went bad fast, the cops stormed in and started arresting people for drugs. I heard the commotion and jumped out the window onto the fire escape. From that moment on I stuck mostly to alcohol.

Keith always used more than me. At any given night, when I stopped, he kept going. He made me feel like my drinking wasn't too bad. After Keith and I lost touch, my drinking got worse. After I got drunk while babysitting my nephew, my sister stopped talking to me. I told my mother, "I can't stop. I don't even like this anymore." She said to pray. I did. I prayed to have the strength to quit and to reconnect with Keith.

I only remember having three vodka tonics. The next thing I knew, I was kissing Buddy while Keith smoked meth across the room. Buddy put his hands down my pants and then removed his hand like he was recoiling from a hot flame. I don't remember much after that. I heard the two of them yelling, and I woke up in a guest room hung over and with Keith sitting on the edge of the bed. He looked haggard and worn, like he hadn't slept in a long time. His skin was dry and grey. His eyes were dull.

"What happened last night?" I asked him. I said "last night" but I didn't have any idea how long I was passed out.

"You had too much to drink, and we took you upstairs," Keith tried to look comforting, but he couldn't hide his sadness. All I wanted was to go back to sleep.

I berated myself for another night of not being able to control my drinking. My two-drink maximum had been working for a couple of months. Now, I was back to square one.

"It's not his fault, you know," Keith said. "I came to him and I've stayed, so it's on me." I vaguely understood that he was talking about his relationship with Buddy. My head was pounding and the light from the crack in the blackout curtains was making my eyes burn. I remembered kissing Buddy the night before. Another thing to a long list of regrets from nights drinking or getting high.

I tried to apologize and comfort him. "Look, I'm sorry I kissed Buddy. You know I don't want him." I suddenly afraid I had done more than just kiss him. "Did anything else happen?" I said a silent prayer.

Keith tried to smile again, but it made me uncomfortable because of how much sorrow was emanating from him. "No. No. That's not what I mean. I just wanted us to see each other again before it's too late."

I let out a sigh of relief. "We will always be friends. You don't have to worry about that." I laid back down with a thud. I felt myself drifting back to sleep, but Keith shook my shoulders trying to wake me up.

"Listen to me," he kept saying.

The temperature dropped noticeably, and I saw a shadow over

Keith's left shoulder. That shadow slowly took shape. I thought I was hallucinating because the shadow started to take the form of Buddy. Then, everything went blank again.

When I opened my eyes again, Keith was talking. "I didn't plan this, you know. Everything happened so fast. At first, it seemed so good, almost too good to be true. Then, it changed before my eyes, but I didn't trust what I saw. I didn't trust myself. It felt so good. Warm, like a plate of freshly baked cookies. I felt free to do whatever I wanted without shame or guilt. I thought I was experiencing my body in full for the first time. Then, I realized I was losing pieces. At first, small pieces and the pieces got bigger, until I was all gone. I'm just a shadow now."

"Baby, you're not making sense," I said. "But if you want out of here, let's go. I will take you back to your mother. She misses you."

Keith touched my face. His hand was cold. He said, "Remember my grandma? She loved you. She thought I should marry you, but that was when she thought you were a girl. When I told her you were really a boy, she looked at me and huffed, 'I don't know about all that. I know you can't get rid of your essence and that person loves you.'"

I was shocked. "You never told me that story before."

"I didn't want to hurt your feelings. She didn't understand stuff like transition, but she never got mad at me for being gay," Keith said.

I was getting mad, not at Keith's grandmother, but at him for never telling me that she thought we were meant to be together. *What if she was right? Maybe we could have been good for each other.*

"Did you ever think your grandmother was right about us? That we should have been a couple?"

Keith looked at me with a tenderness that made me want to hold him and never let go. "I would have pulled you down. You've got a chance. You used to talk about getting sober. You tried to get me to do it, you should take your own advice."

I went to reassure him that it wasn't too late for him but, Keith stopped me. He said, "Promise me you will take care of yourself. Promise me when you leave this house, you will get sober. Promise me," he insisted. I rolled my eyes, but he put his hands on either side of my head and looked me in the eyes so hard, I was afraid to not do what he wanted.

He wouldn't let me go until I said it. "I promise," I said.

We both relaxed. I laid down and pulled Keith on top of me. I wanted him. His lips, his eyes, his hands. There was nothing like the hands of a man on my body. Keith's hands were firm and caring. They explored my body in a way that didn't make me want to cover it up. When I started dating men after transition, I was so afraid. Afraid of being rejected, judged, laughed at. But not with Keith, Keith made me feel special. Not in a spectacle kind of way, but special, like I was the sexiest man he ever met. I tried to feel special like that using tequila or rum. It worked for a while, then it stopped working and I just felt out of control and ashamed. No other man made me feel like a man the way that Keith did. When I saw him on my bed, I instinctively opened like a fan. He made me feel like I belonged with other men. A queer man among other queer men. No one matched him in how he made me feel. Other men were open but reserved. He gave me all of himself every time.

He slid his hands under my shirt and moved across my stomach and then up to my chest. I shivered with pleasure and anticipation of the next stroke. I wanted to feel his lips and tongue on my skin. I pulled him toward me for a kiss and then turned my head slightly to guide his lips to my neck and ear. I shivered as his tongue slid from my earlobe to the nape of my neck, his hands exploring my thighs and ass. Fresh, new touch. Heavy and tight.

I put on my harness and dick and then I put lube on Keith's ass. I started kissing him from the belly button and worked my way down between his legs, then up to his neck. He giggled a little, partly seeming like it was from being ticklish and partly from being nervous. But it sounded different than I had ever heard it before, ethereal, and distant, like his laugh echoed off the corners of the room. Keith guided my attention to sliding my dick inside him and he gasped. I forgot about the laugh and savored the look on his face with each push, how he arched is back and moved his hips, encouraging me to go deeper.

When I was deep inside Keith, rocking with him, and stroking his dick at the same time, I saw Buddy out of the corner of my eye. He was sitting in a chair across the room. I tried to stop and yell at him, but I couldn't stop. Again, Keith pulled my attention back to him. My instinct was to pull out, but instead, I pushed harder and faster. Keith's eyes were closed, as he stroked himself. I knew he was close. This should have been a moment of joy and homecoming, but it felt more like estrangement. I was not in control of my actions. My body didn't feel like mine anymore, and Keith felt farther away than ever.

The room was spinning. When I tried to make sense of things, the faster things spun, and I felt as if I was going to fly off the bed into an abyss. So, I concentrated on staying put. After Keith came, he held me close and wrapped his legs around my waist, which were so heavy that I was trapped on top of him. I turned the few inches I could, to see if Buddy was still there, or really there at all. Then, Keith was gone. He vanished from underneath me. I was overcome by sleep.

I don't know how long I slept, but I dreamt of Buddy in the chair in the room I was sleeping in, and Keith sitting on his lap with his head on Buddy's shoulder. Next in the dream, Keith stood at the entrance to the Lost Wing. He had large, beautiful, white wings that protruded from his shoulder blades. He was wearing tight, white pants, and no shirt. His muscles glistened in the recessed lighting. He was blowing me kisses and waving.

When I woke up, I felt heavy, like I had slept for too long. I went downstairs but I didn't find Buddy or Keith. I went to the Lost Wing. When I opened the curtains, I was met with cold air, not the kind of chill you feel in a drafty old house, but the kind that makes your insides shiver with warning. It was completely dark, as if it were a tunnel.

Before I took another step and I said out loud, "This is for Keith." I could feel someone watching me. I thought I heard breathing in the dark. I groped along the wall for a light switch and found one. When I flipped the switch, I was ready to scream at whoever or whatever was waiting for me. But there was nothing but a long corridor of buzzing fluorescent lights on the ceiling.

"Hello?" I called out, but there was no sound. I wasn't just quiet, but besides my voice, there was an absence of sound. The hall was completely different from anything else I had seen so far. The walls were painted a dull tan color, at least that's what it looked like under the dim florescent lighting. Much of it was chipped and cracked, and there was dust on the floor and walls, as if it had been abandoned for decades. In contrast to the ugly surroundings, the hall smelled pleasantly sweet, like there would be cookies or homemade candy waiting for me in the kitchen, which I knew was back there. The smell seemed familiar, but I couldn't place it. It made me feel more relaxed. I followed it to the kitchen's double doors.

I was shocked. I expected an ultra-modern kitchen with the latest gadgets. Instead, I found a mostly bare room. The walls looked like they were once cream-colored, but years of smoke and grease had left dark smudges and a layer of film. The countertops had not been updated since the 70s. Tan Formica counters were accompanied by dirty, checkered linoleum floors. There were holes in the floors where it looked like the linoleum had crumbled from age and wear. I hadn't seen anything like the stove and refrigerator since I was a kid at my grandmother's house. The fridge was an old-fashioned white one with a small freezer door on top and the stove was old and covered with grease. The floors and countertops were so thick with dirt and dust, I couldn't imagine anyone making food there, which didn't make sense because I saw Buddy come out from behind the curtain with fresh platters of food and drinks. I couldn't imagine those serving trays being in that side of the house without getting smudged with dirt and grime. The dust covered every surface so much that I was concerned that I was going to be smeared with it by the time I left.

Keith said that he was staying in a room in the Lost Wing of the house. I knew I found his room because I could see some of his things in it. His jacket was flung over a chair. On the bed was the baseball cap that he wore when he asked me to leave his ex-boyfriend's house. The room was as shabby as the rest of the wing. It had cardboard on the windows that was secured by masking tape and peeling at the top. In the corners, the tape had lost its glue and sagged under the weight of the cardboard, which was saturated with dirt. A little bit of light peaked through the corners and with the help of the light from the hall, I could see an old single rollaway cot, the kind with the springs that squeak, a desk, one metal folding chair and a lamp. I don't think there were any lights in the ceiling, or at least nothing turned on when I flip the switch. The floor was covered with checkered black and white linoleum squares like the kitchen. The walls had a hideous black and white wallpaper with little spades. It was stripped in places, revealing the paint-chipped wall and wallpaper plaster underneath. It was like some strange, dilapidated bachelor pad from a bygone era. Just under the smell of cookies, there was another scent, something rotten and dense. It was like a thick undercoating and the sweet smell laid on top of it. It sat in the back of my throat, and I couldn't identify it. The odors of cookies and rotting food or flesh ended abruptly at the doorway like an invisible wall. Nothing in the room made sense—the floor, the walls, the lack of order. The whole wing, with its peeling paint and layers of cobwebs, dust and dirt, were so different from the rest of the mansion. Everything made me dizzy and disoriented. I felt something or someone hovering over my right shoulder. I looked around, but no one else was in the room. Yet I couldn't shake the feeling that I was not alone. The hairs on the back of my neck went full attention and everything in my body screamed to leave that room.

For a few seconds, the rest of the house looked like the lost wing. It was neglected and dirty. There were holes in the walls and parts of the ceiling was falling down. Cobwebs covered the chandelier and the corners. The furniture was covered with white sheets and the paintings were of generic landscapes and lighthouses, faded and fallen. Buddy stood at the door to the living room. He was smiling, so warmly, like he was welcoming me home.

"What's the matter, Richard? Can I get you something? Come, sit." I turned towards the door and found myself in bed with nothing but my pants on.

I heard a voice that was something like Buddy's, but lower and gravellier. "Good night," it said.

The first thing that hit me when I woke up was the smell. It was the same sweet smell of homemade cookies and cakes that I had encountered in the Lost Wing, only it was much stronger, and it permeated my body and my mind, wiping out all thoughts, and I felt unable to think about resisting anything or anyone. I could not remember what life was like outside of the house. *Had I arrived the day before, or was it two days?* I put on the only shirt I could find. It was too big for me, which was strange because I usually wore an extra-large and it wasn't that big. Time was slipping from me. I could not remember where I had been before coming to visit Keith or how I got to the house. I knew I came from somewhere else, but where? *My car. I came here in a car.* My hands shook as I tried to open the curtains to see out to the curb. I couldn't bring myself to open the curtains to verify that there was a car outside. *If I came by car that must mean I live close by.* I closed my eyes to try and picture the trip here. I could see lots of buildings and a highway. *Did I live in this city?* I had a vague sense that I was somewhere I should know. I came here in the daylight. That much I knew. The look of the grinning face made by the windows and doors of the house in the sunlight flashed across my mind.

When I looked down, I realized that I didn't recognize the clothes I was wearing. I had on a dirty T-shirt that said, "Dance On," with a picture of a white woman in go-go boots and a miniskirt in silhouette, denim shorts and flip flops. I couldn't remember what I usually wore, but I knew this wasn't it.

I left the room and headed down the stairs toward the living room. That's when I saw it. I hadn't noticed a hidden room between the living room and the lost wing. It was partially hidden behind the velvet curtain, but I saw its incredible whiteness peeking out from behind the royal blue. There seemed to be a white glow coming from it. I pulled back the curtain and walked through the door. In it was what I can only describe as a room glowing with whiteness. The walls were opaque white glass with a light source behind them, making it so bright that I had to let my eyes adjust before I could see Keith. He was lying on a table in white briefs and white socks. Instead of the grey I had seen in his skin when I arrived, he was blue! He was shivering and his lips were blue, and his skin looked as if he had spent the night in a freezer. His eyes were open wide, and he had a wild look in them. As he struggled to speak, I immediately took off my shirt and put it on him, gathering him in my arms. He was warm to the touch, even as he continued to quake. "I...I'm sorry," I heard him whisper with some effort.

"Come on. I'll get you to a hospital," I said.

He was so thin I thought I had a good chance of carrying him out the door into the car with little effort.

"R-r-r-," He was trying to say something else, but I concentrated on opening the door with him cradled in my arms like a baby. I realized too late that he was trying to say, "Run!"

I felt a pinch in my back and then nothing.

I was in a big velvet chair in the living room, facing the curtains to the Lost Wing. Through my haze, I saw Buddy lead Keith and a much younger Black man through the curtain to the Lost Wing. They were followed by two men who look to be in their 50s or 60s. One was white, the other one was Black. I recognized the Black man, but I couldn't put my finger on why. The two men looked at me hungrily, and the white one turned and started to walk my way, when Buddy said, "No, not that one," and led him into the Lost Wing.

I could not say how long I spent going in and out of consciousness. It felt like a few minutes and an eternity at the same time. Each time I opened my eyes, I heard unearthly sounds coming from the side of the house where the three men disappeared. I managed to pull myself up and stumble past the doorway into the forbidden wing. That's when I saw the young Black man on a table. He was positioned on his back naked, limp, with his eyes closed. At first, I thought he was dead, but then I saw his body twitch. His head was hanging off the edge of the table and his legs in the air. Buddy was the most frightening sight. He was standing between the two, his right hand on his dick and the other one on the young Black man's torso. His left hand was slowly melding with the young man's skin, his fingers burrowed into his flesh and stretched out like tentacles. The more his fingers slithered under his skin, the more the young man began to weakly try to push and squirm away. The young man was so vulnerable splayed out for these men to hunt and violate. There he was, barely conscious, his eyes rolled back in his head, lips forced open, his arms weakly slapping them away. The three of them were taking from him to satisfy themselves. The older Black man that I found so familiar was thrusting his dick down the young man's throat, causing him to choke, but he did not fully wake up. I remebered who the Black man was. He was Reverend Williams from a famous mega-church in LA. He was just in the news for leading a rally against gays grooming children where he called for the screening of all homosexuals and gender perverts who are teachers for the propensity towards sexual abuse of children. I remember shaking my head to his face on the news. The betrayal I felt then was magnified 100-fold watching him fulfill his own base desires while the young man's body was limp. The other white man was huffing as he fucked the young man's ass without a condom.

I could not scream. The white man was a given, but the sight of Reverend Williams hurt much more. Witnessing this act made me sick. I felt like I was also on that table, wide open for their pleasure. I called up every bit of strength I could and pulled myself off the chair. It was like walking against the winds of a hurricane. I pushed forward to stop what they were doing and in search for Keith.

I found Keith curled in the corner weeping, his hands shaking as he fixed a needle for his arm. I mustered all the strength I had and shouted at them. Buddy looked at me, his eyes red and bulging. He stopped stroking his dick long enough to wave his arm in my direction. I woke up back on the couch in the living room.

Time was spinning. It seemed as if it were days earlier, before the young man on the table, back on the first night when I drank too much. I couldn't tell if the light was dimmed or my eyes weren't working, but I could barely see. I could just make out what Keith and Buddy were wearing. Everyone was in the same clothes we had on when I first arrived. I overheard them whispering in the dark.

"You knew exactly what would happen if you brought him here."

"That's a lie. I did not. No. No. He's my friend. I wanted to visit with a friend, just this once. That's what I said when I asked if he could stay!" Keith was angry and crying.

"I'm the only friend you'll ever need again," Buddy responded.

"I'm begging you," Keith said like it was a warning.

"What kind of friend are you? You set him up. I'm not responsible for what happens," Buddy sneered.

I managed to pull myself up to say, "No!" but I was back in the white room, facing Buddy and Keith was quivering on the floor.

Buddy was smiling at me, that horrible, confident grin. "He is not a prisoner here," he said, handing Keith a pair of shiny handcuffs.

"Then why are you handing him handcuffs?"

"I will not force him to use the handcuffs. He's going to put them on all by himself. Because he wants to." He turned to look at Keith and said, "If you want him to leave unharmed, put these on and lock yourself to that table over there in the corner."

Keith, now with tears streaming down his face, took the handcuffs and walked over to the corner table. He avoided looking at me in the eyes.

I managed to get to him. "You don't have to do this!" I begged. He pushed me away. "Why don't you leave with me?"

"Forget me, Richard," Keith said, suddenly calm.

I tried to drag Keith out of the room, but he pushed me hard, so hard that I tripped over a red metal tool box that I could not push out of the way. Buddy didn't move. He just stood there watching Keith shackle himself to the wooden table and sit down on the floor, holding on to one of the legs crying. Buddy kicked the large red toolbox over to Keith like it weighed nothing. Keith pulled out a pipe and a baggie that I assumed was filled with meth.

I ran from that house, leaving Keith shackled to the table. I ran directly to the police. They said they would look into it. It took two days of pushing, before they sent a patrol car.

I saw Keith one last time. He was still at Buddy's house.

"Don't believe him," I said to the cops. "A guy was out cold, and they were fucking him. He couldn't consent. Buddy gave him the drugs. And then he did things to him. He is a monster. He put his hand inside his belly and consumed him from the inside out."

One of the cops looked at me and said, "Look, if you don't calm down, I'm going to arrest you."

Buddy smiled at the cop. "I do my best to give them someplace to go, but sometimes it doesn't work out."

I yelled, "I'm not one of his fucking charity cases. Tell them!" I shouted at Keith, but he looked away. "I'm not like them." The words rang hollow in my ears and rattled in my head. What made me hot with anger was Buddy's smile when I said it.

I felt the tension in the room rise. Everything I said was drained of what little credibility it had. The cops looked at each other and dispensed with whatever politeness they mustered before. "Oh yeah, what are you on? Why don't you empty your pockets."

While one of the cops was searching me for drugs, the other explained in an irritated tone, "All we see here is that Mr. Upton was taking care of his sick friend out of the goodness of his heart."

The cops apologized to Buddy and told me that there was no evidence that anyone was being held against their will. They asked Buddy if I were trespassing and if he wanted me escorted off the property.

"There's no need for that. I can handle things from here," he said.

The cops left. "You should have never come back," Buddy said to me, savoring a long drink from his highball. I could not move. My body would not obey my commands. "Now, you will never leave."

Behind him, I could see Keith's face light up with rage. "You promised!" he yelled at Buddy.

"Shut up," Buddy scolded him, while never taking his eyes off me. He was ten feet away, but I could feel him reaching down inside me. Keith picked up a candelabra from the grand piano in the living room. I didn't see what he did, but the candles were suddenly fully lit. He touched the flames to the velvet curtains at the entrance of the

Lost Wing. Buddy whipped around, but it was too late. The fire was already spreading. He lunged at Keith, knocking him to the ground. The two of them fought, as the fire stretched across the walls. The fire danced between the velvet-covered furniture onto the wooden tables. The room once again looked as if it had been abandoned for decades. Despite my terror of the fire, I tried to make my way across the room to pull Keith out. I didn't make it very far when, from behind the burning curtain, came a small army of Black men. All of them were in white underwear. Some were wearing white T-shirts and knee socks. All of them were focused on Buddy. They grabbed him off Keith and dragged him toward the Lost Wing, as he thrashed around like a bug suddenly caught on its back. Keith got up and even though I called for him to follow me, he also went toward the Lost Wing, which was now a corridor of flames. The last thing he did was look at me and blow me a kiss before he turned and followed the others down the hall.

I did not hear the firefighters as they smashed through the front of the house, but I felt them pull me out of the grinning doors. I told them about Keith and Buddy and the other men, but they said they found no one else in the house. I think the thing that kept me from being blamed for the fire was that they found the red toolbox intact and filled with the drugs I said were in it, clearly marked, "Property of Buddy Upton."

ACKNOWLEDGEMENTS

Maferefun Oshun! Maferefun Oya! Maferefun Shango! Maferefun Orisha!

I would like to acknowledge all the love and care I have received from my family: Omi, Nia, Sydney, Marcus, Michael, and Kevin.

Thank you to those who read this manuscript and gave feedback: Xavier Livermon, Terrance Wooten, Christopher McAuley, Courtney Morris, and Omise'eke Tinsley.

Thank you to Tranogress Press editor and publisher Trystan Cotten for his openness and attention to detail.

Made in the USA
Columbia, SC
07 February 2025

52757989R00078